MUST
BE
DREAMIN'

Wattle Tree Press
www.wattletreepress.com
ABN 55 778 838 320

A catalogue record for this book is available from the National Library of Australia

Must Be Dreamin'
ISBN (paperback): 978-0-6456910-8-5
ISBN (ebook): 978-0-6456910-9-2

Cover design: Wattle Tree Press
Typesetting: Wattle Tree Press
Compiled by: Brooke DeBono

Wattle Tree Press wishes to acknowledge the first storytellers across the vast land of Australia, on which we live, work, and dream. From the oral stories told by our ancestors, to the descendants who write them down for future generations to enjoy, we pay our respects to those whose continued cultural and spiritual connections to Country shape our world today, and recognise their valuable contributions to our society.

*For all those whose dreams are
as big and vast as the sky is blue.*

MUST BE DREAMIN'

AN AUSTRALIAN ANTHOLOGY

Contents

Foreword

Dreaming is an important concept here in Australia. It's not just a nighttime activity, or a goal set for the future – dreams thrive in our country as more than imagination.

Dreaming brings to mind a connection to an ancestral past, and a link between past, present, and future.

The idea of DREAMING is important and lasting.

Dreaming is culture – the mystical allure of the Dreamtime, to more modern aspirations.

Dreaming is landscape – the earth drawn in story on ancient stone, the darkened dreamscapes of nightly reveries, and the boundless potential of waking aspirations in this vast and lucky country we call home.

Dreaming is in the mind and in the body – whether in a cultural, psychological, subconscious, or aspirational sense, dreaming invokes scientific inquiry and personal reflection.

Dreaming, as a concept, remains a captivating and essential aspect of the human experience. It transcends time, shaping our narratives and connecting us to the essence of who we are, what we want, and how we wish the world might be.

Here at Wattle Tree Press we live on dreams. We thrive on imagination and love deep dives into the creative minds of others. We believe Australia isn't just the lucky country – it's the home of big dreamers, big ideas, and big hearts.

This anthology invites you to tap into the eternal spirit of dreams, with each author weaving their words to capture the essence of dreaming – from the mystical to the mundane.

We invite you into our dreams, and those of our authors, who each won a place for publication in this anthology.

Keep reading.

Keep writing.

Keep dreaming.

Natalie Bock

Natalie Bock is a word addict who composes poetry and prose. A scribbler since she learned to write, she paused to raise her sons before returning to the writing scene in 2022. Since then, to her continuing astonishment, her words have found their way into five anthologies and a collection of short stories and won a poetry award. Natalie hopes never to wake from this delightful dream come true.

Morning Mystery

by Natalie Bock

I woke with a gemstone stuck to my stomach.
Silver, sparkling, sticky-backed, shining against my skin.
Where did it come from if it wasn't there last night?
Did my darling decorate me during my dreaming?
Did the faery folk kiss me as I succumbed to slumber,
deep in that place where the veil is thin
between their world and ours?
Or was it simply stuck to a sheet,
transferring to my torso as I tossed and twisted and turned?
But ... the sheets had been on the bed a week.
Pyjama pants and an overlapping top
covered my body against the cold.
Yet I woke sensing something was different –
A peek in the mirror confirming what my fingers felt.
I went to sleep with my skin unadorned.
I woke with a gemstone stuck to my stomach.

Glenda Morgan

Glenda Morgan is a poet and artist who resides on Yuin Country in Bermagui NSW. Her Chinese/Indigenous/Irish heritage influences her writing, creating refreshing connections to self and Earth. As an emerging poet, Glenda is an advocate for the previously unnoticed and neglected.

A Day in Dream

by Glenda Morgan

Driving into town
from bright clear non-there air
the car dives into white mystery,
a slow preamble of spindrift, a
salt filled blanket that drapes over
houses, put away from another day.

Familiar streets take on faded edges,
stillness as if permanent, pouring
leftover winter from ocean tides
while
inland, between mountains, cloud drifts
are captured in valley beds,
through soft gelatine rivers. Look
to the lover – the mist – elusive
as it searches for its coastal rarity.

Summer fog
over my left shoulder, flat shining
water in its terrestrial womb
sways with bliss
tumbling grey creeping sideways
mounding clouds, a shadowing
over my right shoulder.

The birth of morning.
A band of gold rises so softly.
my marriage ring finger reaches
to meet this slash of gods' thoughts
light – a knife edge flashes –
between sea and sky
an introduction, perhaps, to the troubles
of divinity or a golden moment of dreams.

Jess Senff

Jessica Senff writes MG and YA fantasy novels based in magical worlds and featuring strong young characters facing a variety of unique problems ... often involving evil sorcery! She loves when these individuals prevail, reminding the reader that solutions can often be found in life – with a little perseverance and good humour.

Must Be Dreamin'

by Jess Senff

"Ye must be dreamin', son!" My dad's croaked voice shot at me over the chug of the engine, our run-down Toyota Landcruiser sputtering its way along the red dirt road.

I clutched the application form on my lap, its gleaming white pages becoming rumpled beneath the weight of humidity and perspiration. A film of dust was sifting its way through the open windows, colouring everything it touched that same rusty red.

"It's a *really* good program, Dad. And there's a scholarship, and everything! You and Mum won't have to *pay* a thing ..." I protested weakly, hateful tears brimming in my eyes.

The Robotics camp was *hours* away, up in the big city. Here, out in the middle of woop-woop, in the back of some one-pub town, the notion of seeing the flashy lights and towering buildings of civilisation really *was* only a dream. Because getting there was a headache in logistics. The drive to the nearest airport was about six hours, and even then you had to catch a puddle-jumper to the closest big town. After that, a bigger plane would take you the rest of the way to the city.

For a country kid whose furthest trip was an hour down the road to the property boundary that sported a crooked barbed wire fence and a letter box attached to a half-rotted tree stump, it was the most exciting of dreams.

I glared out the window as I stuffed the thick glossy forms back into their freshly torn envelope to protect them from the invading dirt.

"It's not the money, son! I just don't want to see ye disappointed, lad." the old man croaked, a durry hanging from one corner of his lips, cooling ash sprinkling off the smoking end as he spoke. "It's a competitive thing, that Robotics camp. There's no real guarantee ye'll even get in. Then, if ye do, ye'll be gone for *weeks*! Ye mum will miss ye, and ye nan. Ye probably will be homesick, and then what? And, who's to help bring the cattle in when Old Marley's up with the road train, aye? I need the extra hands, ye know that."

I glowered at those crooked hands, swollen with arthritis and scarred from hard labour, clasping the steering wheel with confident ease. Guilt constricted my chest for a moment, making it hard to draw a full breath. Dad wasn't as spry as he used to be.

No. His reluctance was about the *station*.

It was *always* about the station.

Who was going to make notes during the livestock inspections? I was a right hand at tapping out the information on my tablet and air-dropping the file onto Dad's laptop when the day was done.

Who else was going to hop on the UTV and muster the cattle to the next paddock every morning, cycling the livestock so no one area was over grazed?

It wasn't that we didn't have the money to put on more station hands, but reliable workers just weren't around anymore. Outside of the family, that is. I mean, it never used to *just* be me. I had bigger brothers, and a sister. But they had all moved on for now.

Wendy was married and living some eight hours drive away on the big dairy farm south-east of us. Tommy was her twin, and they had always been close, so he upped and moved with her when the new husband offered him a job as his dairy manager. Brandon was chasing dinosaur bones with the university he now attended, and Glenn ... Well, no-one had really heard much from Glenn since he and Dad had an all-up knock-out yelling match which led to him taking off as a roaming Drover ...

Times had certainly changed.

Back when we were all together, and Dad was younger and his joints didn't crunch and crackle the way they did now, when he had the three older boys helping him, I had all the freedom in the world to play with my gadgets. Wires, batteries, lights, electric motors ...

Dad used to never care how many hours I spent on my toys, just so long as I did well at my online schooling.

I was just ... so ... *bored!*

That was why my science teacher, Mister Rochester, had posted me this application. The Robotics camp was a chance to challenge myself. To live a life that wasn't dry red dust, cracked earth, spindly grass, and an endless bowl of searing blue sky.

The rest of the car trip was quiet, with only the rough motor rumbling away as we jounced over rocks and around divots in the rutted road. What was the point in arguing? Dad never let up once his mind was made.

I blinked away the angry, helpless tears as the old truck rattled across the cattle grate imbedded in the ground at the boundary to the home paddock.

"Hop out and get the gate, Coop," Dad muttered, casting me a stern look, as though waiting for me to argue or offer up attitude.

Gritting my teeth, I pushed the rusty door open and hopped down onto the uneven ground, my boots thumping up a plume of dust as they made contact. The steel gate was latched shut with a small chain fastened to another of those rotted-tree-stumps and only took a moment to undo. I swung the broad metal frame open with a skip and a jump that had me land on the bottom rung, my weight sending it gliding over rock and soil to clang noisily against the adjacent fence.

The Landcruiser growled its way through and I reversed the swing and latched the gate securely closed once more.

"Ye wanna hop back in?" Dad called from the driver's window.

"Nah, I'll walk." I called back, grubby envelope still clutched in one hand.

The old man saluted me with one finger to the brim of his worn Akubra before he accelerated away, the truck backfiring as it went.

I shook my head, aching to get under the hood and fix whatever engine trouble the tired old vehicle had. Only, Dad didn't trust me enough to know what I was doing. If the truck died, then that would put a right kink in the day-to-day running of the station. The risk wasn't worth it.

I kicked a rock on my way, dawdling as I trudged up the road to the main house. The sun was making its way down the cloudless sky, causing that pristine blue to change into shades of orange and pink.

How was I going to convince Dad to let me go to this camp? Was there any point in even *trying* to change his mind?

As I approached the homestead, I noticed a strange dusty ute parked on the far side near the water tanks.

"Hello! Who's that?" I asked myself as I quickened my pace, practically running for the front door now, my chest filled with excitement and curiosity.

We *never* got visitors out here! Who on earth could have shown up when Dad and I had been out collecting the mail? I didn't notice anyone coming in the main gate ...

Which meant they would have had to come from the western side. So it was someone who knew the area and could get around. A local. Or ...

I burst into the living room, the squeaky screen door with its torn flyscreen slamming closed behind me.

"Glenn!" I squeaked in surprise.

"Hey Bruh, how you going?" He grinned at me, his teeth straight and white against his tanned face.

His blue eyes were twinkling just as I remembered them, although he had a dark beard now that matched his wild tangle of walnut hair.

"Fine! Great!" I gasped.

"Slow down, mate! Take it easy. I ain't going nowhere." The man laughed softly as I threw myself into his arms, hugging him hard around the middle.

Glenn had been the one that taught me to ride my first horse. And my pee-wee motorbike, and the ATV. He helped me with my maths homework, and had even showed me the basics for robotics. He was the reason I was so passionate about all things mechanical.

"What are you *doing* here?" I rasped, blinking back tears.

"Oh, you know. Nan and I talk sometimes, and she was saying that Dad needed some help around the station. You know. Cos you were heading off to the coast to attend some flashy camp and learn more about those robots you're always making," he replied, his grin broadening as my jaw dropped in incredulous joy.

"What? Are you *serious?!*" I gaped up at him.

Dad stood there with a sour look on his face, but said nothing in protest. Mum beamed at me, happy tears in her eyes. Nan, bless her loving soul, wrapped me in her arms and whispered in my ear. "This is your dream, poppet. So, whatever you do, you just keep dreamin'."

Sandra Taylor

Sandra Taylor, writing of earth, heart and spirit, has a BA in Professional Writing and works within the community on art, theatre, and poetry projects. Living in a forest in a mud brick castle immersed in birdsong, Sandra Taylor plays, creatively exploring the sacred and the mundane.

Colonial Outlaw

by Sandra Taylor

all for the 'gentleman's thrill of killing'
dear fox
you were ripped
from your homeland, dragged over the
ocean
now an adept, racing like wind on
borrowed ground
still hunted, baited,
shot
and vilified
by common consensus.
venetian slats morning light
shadowing the thin membrane of ocular
vision dragging consciousness out of repose.
a teasing white tipped tail disappears back
through nights' portal
orange red gold winter fur thick

I remember then in that moment of almost here
a recurring childhood dream:
running
small legs pumping

chest heaving
a stitch in my side
feeling scared
ginger fox nipping at my heels
tumbling into the red telephone box on the corner of reynolds and
milne
breathless
safe
staring through the glass door
yellow eyes, hazel, both of us feral, grinning

later that morning from a den in the
creek bank opposite, ginger
fox emerges.
yellow eyes swivel
recognition flares.

cunning trickster challenging me to grow
confront my fear
tracking me across the ditch unto this forest
onto my knees teaching
how to live stranger with foreign land
how to hear the calling of
my soul

loyal boon companion
staunch ally
takes no prisoners
dear fox

Paris Rosemont

Paris Rosemont is an Asian-Australian poet with a niche in theatrical performance poetry. Her debut poetry collection *Banana Girl* has been shortlisted for numerous poetry Awards in Australia, Greece and the UK, and awarded 'Distinguished Favorite' in the NYC Independent Press Award 2025.

In Another Life
~Bluebeard's Last Wife

by Paris Rosemont

Start your fairytale afresh
what could have been
in the land of dreams?

Already starting to vanish
before forcibly

        trying to erase

all traces
of her

       new life, new ...

subtle retractions
here   and   there

        almost imperceptible

sensing it anyway
you kiss her doubts away
her warning bells quelled;

      false alarm!

She disregards
her insistent amygdala
persistently tapping
its morse code

. . . − − − . . .

        something is off-kilter!

so besotted

        she did not see it coming

              one fine, sunny day you
              blew that pretty little heart
                  to smithereens

How she bled
for weeks she wept red
soiled all your furniture
everything you touched
turned not Midas-gold
but the colour
of
corrosion
hiring a clean-up crew
to fix this mess
scouring away the grime
erasing the crime
[delete: ~~from your memory~~]
till everything sparkled meticulous-clean
[achieved: spotless mind]

you could not bring yourself
to shove her in the dark

        with skeletons of lovers past

                you keep her locked away
                   in a secret chamber
                 she haunts your dreams

There you must meet
all past and future scrubbed clean
this paradise of joint imagining

C.J. Garth

C.J. Garth has always been captivated by the thrill of adventure and the magic of flight. With a passion for storytelling, CJ enjoys weaving tales that spark curiosity and wonder. Whether exploring the skies in stories or immersing herself in the worlds of others, C.J. finds joy in the power of storytelling to inspire new experiences.

Dawn of Flight

by C.J. Garth

It was the sensation of melting that Phee swore she would never get used to. Her mother said that she never noticed it anymore.

Changing forms was new to Phee, but it was the coolest part about stupid early puberty. She'd gotten the rough end of the family's genetic stick with her womanhood being biologically thrust upon her at an earlier-than-average age of thirty-three.

Most gifts became known around the fiftieth year when the Glyn were considered mature and the base body biologically set so that returning to it was second nature. Glyn were strongly advised not to change earlier than that, due to the pain, and returning became harder as the body struggled to remember its form.

Some early emergers had been unable to return to their base forms at all, sometimes stuck in a half-half body causing issues for the rest of their painful lives.

Despite this hardship, her sister, Alexia, was already nearing a late-bloomer at sixty-five, with none of the signs. Phee knew Alexia was annoyed that her baby sister had beaten her and inherited their mother's gift.

There was no guarantee that she would inherit *any* gifts, thanks to their loving father, who while being Glyn, had never presented with any talent other than the longevity of their race.

Gifts had been anticipated and expected in their family line ... until Phee's great-grandfather, Glaranne, died at six hundred without showing a single one.

It had been such a scandal!

Was he fully of the Glyn? Had his mother been tricked and taken advantage of by a lesser fae, or worse ... a mortal?!

Family lore stated that fewer and fewer Glyn were inheriting their family gifts, but the High Council was hiding this, lest they lose face with the surrounding mortal communities, who had a tenuous peace with the Glyn.

Phee returned her mind to her present situation, trying to remind her body of the form she wanted to take. It might not be perfect; she would need to add more biology books to her growing list of pressing study materials.

The melting sensation turned into a flowing warmth that formed wings from her shoulder blades and skitters across her skin to grow feathers that shone an array of reds and oranges rivalling the colours of the sunrise. Her bones lengthened, hollowing to allow lightness and her muscles prepared the strength to carry her body skyward while keeping a basic humanoid form.

Mother had warned that flying took years of instruction, with most theory learned beforehand in lessons. Phee had been too young to attend those lessons, instead simply lectured on the dangers of trying to fly before the body was ready. Some emergers didn't understand their gifts and permanently damaged themselves.

Like that risk would stop Phee.

She had been gifted wings and the slight inconvenience of not knowing the theory on how to use them would not stop her trying.

The freedom of the sky sung to her very soul, calling her skyward.

As her body's final changes solidified in place, she winced. She hadn't changed many times, due to the pain and warnings from the High Council.

Phee looked at her body in the glass of the small attic window she often used to climb onto the roof and watch the sunrise.

Her legs and torso had elongated, sprouting fine downy feathers that she assumed was to trap body heat when she flew at higher altitudes. Around her bellybutton, the feathers lengthened. She glimmered ombre, colour changing from the oranges near her feet to the deep reddish-purples that framed her face and dark hair.

From her back, the most stunning wings had sprouted. They were long and lean, sloping up past her ears with hand-sized feathers as they approach the ends. The added height meant she would tower over her father now, instead of her usual short stature.

Phee decided that, surely, it wouldn't be too bad if she jumped off the roof of their house. After all, they had done it many times as children, with sheets tied around their shoulders, pretending they had sprouted their mothers' wings. The vegetable garden beds outside the modest building had suffered, but not once had they been seriously hurt.

She was older now.

The drop was not much further than her new willowy height and surely any physical damage would be repaired when she morphed back to her base form.

Drawing a quick breath, she distracted herself from the voice in the back of her head that screamed "Danger!" and warned her how much of a bad idea this was.

Phee ran towards the sky, willing her wings outward, in the manner she had witnessed her mother use when taking flight. She'd seen it numerous times as a child, after sneaking from her bed to spy, then dream of flying off with her mother.

The ground rushed towards her too quickly.

Something had gone wrong.

But the drop was too short for Phee's brain to kick in and figure out how to fix it. Luckily her brother, Ziax, had tended to and harvested the carrots the day before, leaving the garden bed somewhat soft to land in.

Dull pain emerged in all parts of Phee's body.

Brushing the dirt off, she indignantly looked back to the roof, tempted to try again.

The spire from the worship hall stood tall and proud, calling to her as if summoning. Some other emergers, she knew, had used the sacred space to encourage their gifts to fully emerge, and coax out their specific family gifts. The spire was higher, but also more public – not many were awake at this hour, but it could lead to trouble if her mother noticed what she was trying.

Stumbling out of the vegetable plot, still not used to the extra length in her stride, Phee stopped to shake the soil from her feathers. It was an odd sensation to feel them lift and ruffle the dirt from the tiny spaces between them and her sun-kissed skin. It sent shivers along her whole body.

Phee scanned the house, making sure that her tumble hadn't woken her family. Sensing quiet and holding onto the fence for support on newly formed legs, she made her way to the gate, then onto the street.

The walk to the worship hall would have been faster if Phee had reverted to her base form, but that didn't occur to her until she was at the steps to the great oak doors, holding her breath so that the strangled panting of the uphill journey didn't wake any sleeping clerics with auditory gifts.

If they heard her, they'd try to stop her. Luckily, they hadn't.

Phee snuck into the worship hall and to the staircase that would lead her higher, taking the stairs multiple at a time with her new long legs. The climb went quickly.

The sun rising much higher, sure to wake the village soon, which would surely get her caught.

She hurried on.

The spire had a bank of openings and windows around the tallest point before the tapered roof, where the visually gifted watched during times of unrest with the mortals to ensure that the village was safe.

Using an opening on the opposite side of the spire to her house – which would hopefully hide her actions from her mother – Phee climbed over the ledge and stepped to the fine edge that ran along the spire. It was designed to allow flyers to launch in the protection of their village.

She hoped that this attempt would work better than the last, lest she make her own grave amongst her kin below.

Deciding that looking down wasn't the best option, she instead lifted her face to the low sun, listening to its siren call, and stepped off the ledge.

Air rushed by.

Phee realised she hadn't opened her wings. Trying to open them now resulted in catching an updraft and Phee didn't have the strength to right them. Her wings flapped limply behind her head.

The frigid wind rushed past her face, stealing the sobs and screams from her chest and causing her hair to catch in her eyes and mouth, blocking the view of how fast the ground was rushing towards her.

Just as Phee was making peace with her ancestors, an explosion of blue flame overtook her vision.

She felt her feathers tingle, her skin crawling with something ... *new*.

Not a melting, exactly, but something similar to sunburn heated her skin as Phee's true form emerged ...

A phoenix!

The heat radiating from her form lifted her wings.

And.

She.

Soared.

The Sisterhood
of the
Travelling Story

The Sisterhood of the Travelling Story is comprised of five long-term best friends who have been separated by the demands of adulthood, motherhood, and life beyond high school. The Sisterhood became a long-distance book club, then a collaborative writing group during the Covid lockdown era. Each sister would add a few hundred words before sending the story on to the next sister in the chain, to stay connected, creative, and to escape into magical worlds of their own creation.

Finding Steve

by The Sisterhood of the Travelling Story

~ **Part One** ~

Chapter One

Sister 1

It is a truth, universally acknowledged, that a wizard is a hairy, solitary creature cloaked in mystery, magic, and a long dress. He is old and grey, with a hint of mischief and a dash of old-timey charm. "A wizard," his father had said, "was a wondrous thing to be." His father, he had learned early on, was full of codswallop.

For one thing, wizards had beards! Ever seen a clean shaven thousand-year-old magician? No. Because they don't exist. He stroked the wiry, disappointing growth upon his chin – 500 years for five millimeters of sparse, crinkled sprouts.

Another thing – wizards had ancient names as craggy as the hills. Names as mysterious as the mist curling in the valleys. Gandalf. Dumbledore. Merlin. *Wizards are not*, he shuddered at the thought, *named Steve.*

"Like a giant stone in one's path, you must accept and overcome the obstacle." Another pearl of his father's wisdoms that simply did not help.

To date, he had spent countless nights embroiled in sleepless, name-filled frenzies.

Steve.

No wizard was called Steve!

What's more, real wizards had glorious staffs, not a horrid little cane to hobble around on. But that wasn't his fault, it was Gyn's. (Now *there* is a *REAL* wizard's name!)

His older brother liked to play rough, Steve's ankle broken numerous times in their few hundred years under their father's godforsaken roof. Magic, it seemed, could only mend so much.

He dreamed too much to sleep, tormented by his want for good company. Yet, that was another elusive. *Did you ever,* he asked himself often, *hear of a wizard with a wife?* Most were solitary men, not warmed by the friendship and faithfulness of a companion.

Often wishing he'd been someone else, something else, Steve found the time, (in the miniscule hours between his father's lofty rants, his brothers unwanted attention, and their pressing social engagements at Farrenbourn, where the magical society congressed) to learn the art of transfiguration.

Taking the form of a cat, one sore ankle in four didn't seem so utterly bad.

Positively feline, sleek and black as the velvety night itself, Steve snuck out, searching for freedom and friendship.

Slinking into the alley beyond his grand home at Wickton Hall, he slunk into depths of the maze-like garden where he knew (from long experience) that he could steal a few moments. Away from the ballroom, Steve might avoid the pressures of his father's high-society life. And a few moments before Gyn would stalk out to find him.

Nestling into the curled hollow of the tree, where he often curled to read, he murmured, "Teantro!"

A steaming cup of tea appeared. Steve lapped it cautiously with his rough cat's tongue, unimpressed. Sighing, he morphed back into a man.

A strange noise erupted from the acclaimed Wisteria Walk. Ignoring it, Steve refocused on his novel and the steaming brew.

The noise came again.

What is that? ...

Chapter Two

Sister 2

If his brother's unprovoked brutality had taught Steve anything, it was to protect himself. Swiftly, he returned to his feline form and, tea forgotten, curled into the shadows, surveying the area.

He noticed a sleek white fox quickly weave its way through a flowerbed and make a run for a gnarled bush. Not far away, the noise came again and, startled, the fox looked around, its piercing blue eyes locking with his in the shadows. It burnt into him, as if it was reading his mind, before quickly slinking off into the unknown.

Steve contemplated following it. Surely with eyes like that, it had to be another magical being, right? As he was unfurling his body to follow the fox, a green spark passed right in front of his tree. It crashed into his forgotten teacup, smashing the delicate china to charred pieces and smoke. He knew that magic ... Gyn.

Gyn stumbled through the trees of the Wisteria Walk, breaking branches as he followed the path of the shrieking orb to the smouldering teacup. He shouldn't be using magic while drinking, but that had never really stopped him before.

Steve worried that the fox had been the target of the attack, but he could never be quite sure of anything when Gyn was involved. His brother could have been flinging spells for the sheer joy that the destruction brought him.

There was no sign of the fox, so he sought more shadows, hoping that Gyn was passing through on his way to a whichever nymph had somehow fallen for his advances this week. He hoped, too, that his teacup hadn't been a deliberate target, but a part of the general demolition of Steve's things that seemed to follow in Gyn's wake.

Luck was not on his side tonight, unfortunately.

"Tea? Really, Steve?" Gyn stared down at the remains of the teacup. "There's a party inside with the finest food and drink in the realm, and you'd rather sit in a damp hole in a tree and read a book? No wonder everyone thinks you're a loser."

He shouted, flinging another green ball into the distance. It struck a cement vase, exploding it into a burst of flames and smoke. The broken remains fell from its pedestal to form an ashy pile. Steve stayed still. Silent. A shadow.

Sighing, Gyn waved his hand and reversed the damage. After all, he wouldn't want to ruin his sparkly reputation. Gyn was everyone's favourite. Always had been. Steve had no idea why.

Gyn looked around, trying to spot his brother.

This part of the garden offered some coverage, but there weren't a lot of places to hide ...

Chapter Three

Sister 3

Steve tried his best to curl tighter into his mediocre hiding place, shutting his eyes and hoping that if he stayed still enough, Gyn might just lose interest.

Of course, he didn't.

That would've been too convenient.

"Aha!" Steve felt rough hands grab him around the middle and wrench him from the hollow, holding him high in the air. "Hey, Kitty! Come and play! Here, kittykittykitty!"

Gyn laughed at his own apparent hilarity, waving Steve around the garden. Steve slumped, limp in his hands. Like they hadn't been doing this for the past 300 years. It was almost boring, really.

And here comes the part where he tries to take me back to the party and force me to change back into a human. Naked. In front of everyone, Steve thought. *They've all seen it before anyway.*

"Come on Stevie, let's go back to the party! I'm sure everyone wants to see you." Gyn tucked cat-Steve under his arm with a smirk. Steve meowed a resigned sigh.

Just then, a giggle floated to them on the breeze, from the other side of the hedge, followed by a lower, rumbling chuckle. A rustling of the leaves.

Perking up a little, Gyn waved his hand in front of the hedge, which obligingly faded to semi-transparency, revealing a couple clearly out for a moonlit canoodle. Gyn appraised them with a glint in his eye and Steve took this momentary distraction to quickly slip from his brother's grasp.

Darting into the depths of a large, sculpted bush, he turned back just in time to see Gyn give up the look of irritation shooting his way, and move towards the party goers, choosing to join them instead of remain in the dark with his feline sibling.

Steve rolled his eyes, trying to stamp down the envy clutching at his heart. Gyn, for some reason Steve would never understand, had friends. He had female friends, too.

I just wish someone might, even once, give some kind of indication they'd like to share their life with me. Someone I could actually just be myself with, he thought, abandoning his book and the hopes for a quiet night.

He began to slink away under the bush, resolving that he might as well go back to the old plant pot where he'd stashed his clothes, go human again and just call it a night.

Nobody would notice if he didn't return to the ballroom. They were his father's guests, and Gyn's friends, not his.

He looped around the back of the old garden shed, picking his way through the old pots, broken statues, and other long-forgotten outdoor things nobody seemed to know what to do with.

His pity party was interrupted by a gleam of white in his peripheral. He whipped around.

There!

Gleaming in the moonlight, watching him with those vivid blue eyes – The white fox! It sat on a little stone bench that had been carelessly added to junk pile. Steve stopped, rooted to the spot, captivated by the fox's steady gaze.

Those eyes! They held their own magic, and not the kind in Steve's books.

His mind was racing. No one ever came to this part of the garden, which is why Steve hid his human clothes here when taking a feline form. He'd assumed nobody else knew it existed. Why was the fox here? Why? And WHO WAS IT? Because on second, closer viewing, Steve was sure that this was no ordinary fox.

It remained still, watching him, blinking occasionally.

Steve took a few tentative, slow (but deliberate) steps towards it. Did that fox just raise an eyebrow? Do foxes have eyebrows?

Two more steps.

Another.

The fox cocked its head to the side, like a curious puppy, but with an obvious challenge in its eye. Steve began to slowly, but steadily, close the remaining few metres between them.

~ **Part Two** ~

Chapter Four

Sister 4

Steve could feel his heart beating.

Thump. Thump.

Panic rose as he got closer.

What would happen when he reached the creature? Would it run? Would it attack?

Somehow, it didn't matter. He just had to be close to it.

He felt a pull, like the fox were a magnet and he was its counterpart. It was strange and new, but he felt a sense of importance. Destiny, even.

Thump. Thump.

He was only a meter away now. Their eyes still locked. The fox's head was still cocked to one side, assessing his intentions but clearly not concerned by his approach. Steve noted a hint of amusement in its expression. That was slightly annoying.

Now he was closer, he could see the white fur had a blue tinge, matching those piercing eyes. Unblinking eyes. And somehow it seemed to be surrounded by a soft glow of warm, blue light.

Thump. Thump.

He wondered if the fox could hear his heavy heartbeat, too.

Half a meter.

Steve stopped short.

He wasn't sure what to do now he had gotten so close.

They stayed, eyes locked, unblinking, for what seemed like an eternity. The blue eyes burning into his, mesmerising him, hypnotising him.

What was happening? He was 500 years old, for goddess' sake, and a magician to boot!

An unseen, unspoken force was compelling him, and there was nothing he could do but answer to the pull he felt deep inside.

"I have searched many lands and witnessed many moons on my journey to find you."

Steve would have been shocked by the voice in his head if the words hadn't washed over him like warm honey, soothing his very soul with each uttered word. He felt his body tingle from his head to his toes, every black cat hair standing on end as the fox "spoke" to him.

At least, he thought it was the fox. Its mouth didn't move. But its expressions and body language matched the voice that he heard in his head.

Was telepathy a thing? He knew from the start this wasn't your garden variety common fox, but was it magical? Or was this another one of Gyn's pranks? Or (more likely, Steve thought) had he finally gone mad?

500 years of the same old monotony, watching people come and go … immortality can take its toll, eviscerating dreams unachieved and hollowing one's soul, if he wasn't careful about such things.

"Your name is Steve," it said, taking time to pronounce his name.

Steve thought he saw the fox's lip curl up slightly on one side as it mentally spoke the word, as though it, too, believed "Steve" was not a name befitting a wizard.

This time, he noted the voice in his head was unmistakably female. It was a soft, deep drawl that made his mind feel like he was being enveloped by clouds. His body warmed and relaxed. Even his chronic ankle pain seemed to melt away.

If he was in his human form, his expression would have been one of pure confusion and disbelief. He didn't understand what was happening. He wasn't afraid, though he knew he should have been. This was an entirely alien experience for him. Why wasn't he even the slightest bit concerned about this?

"Yes, I'm Steve. Who are you? WHAT are you?" he asked tentatively. He spoke out loud, not sure if he was mad, if he could project his thoughts, or even if the fox would understand him. To his surprise and relief, she answered.

"I am a guardian." Her expression remained gentle, her ears pricked forward, and her eyes still locked on his.

Chapter Five

Sister 5

"My name is Fleur. And I'm here to ask you for your help."

Steve stood in silence, shocked that, of all the wizards in the realm, somebody would need his help. There was a whole ballroom of magical people in the grand house beyond, but the fox – Fleur – wanted *him?*

Steve's mouth dried, and his voice came out in harsh croaks.

"Me? Are you sure you have the right wizard?"

The fox continued to stare at him with those piercing eyes, as if she could see into his soul.

"Yes," she said firmly. "Will you come with me or not?"

Steve could still hear the commotion of his brother close by, and he shuddered at the thought of having to go back to that party, to watch Gyn strut about and blabber on.

He wasn't a very adventurous wizard, preferring to spend his days pouring over scrolls and books in the great library. But something within Steve was pulling him toward Fleur.

Determined, he shifted into human form and darted behind the plant pot where his clothes were stashed. Quickly, he pulled on his pants and boots, still struggling into his shirt when tinkling laughter filled his ears and the fox began to move.

"Come, let's go!"

Steve's feet followed her without even pausing to consider where they might be going.

They rounded the shed and followed a path towards the servants' quarters. The shrubs were overgrown and blocked the view of the path ahead.

Steve could barely see the flicking blueish-white tail of the fox moving swiftly down the path. He tried to hurry, but the bushes seemed to be getting thicker and pushing in against him.

Turning his face to the side, he narrowly avoided a particularly thorny branch, tripping slightly. Stumbling forward, he threw out his arm to catch himself, but his hands were caught by someone else's.

They were smaller than his, soft and warm, with skin pale as moonlight.

Looking down, he found that the ground was now a thick carpet.

There must have been a portal and he clumsily fell right through it!

Steve quickly glanced around. He was standing in front of a large fireplace in a room filled with bookshelves (he'd fallen into Heaven?!). Thick drapes covered the windows and a table to his left was piled high with scrolls and tomes that cried out for his attention.

The hands holding his seemed to sense his awe. They squeezed gently, bringing his attention back from the parchment. His gaze drifted from the hands, up the arms and came to rest on the smiling face of a woman.

Steve let out an audible gulp as he beheld Fleur's human form, as alluring as her animal one.

Those same bewildered blue fox eyes were set wide in a soft round face. Her long hair, as white as the fox's coat, hung freely over her shoulders. She was wearing a midnight blue velvet dress, with a wide brown leather belt. A short sword hung from the belt in a well-loved scabbard.

When Fleur let him go, her hand came to rest comfortably on the hilt, as if this was where it belonged.

Chapter Six

Sister 1 (again)

Looking around the small, stone-walled cabin, he smiled familiarly at the book spines – copies of the worn titles he'd read so frequently and feverishly in his isolation. Running a hand over his shamelessly beardless face, Steve leant on the grand wingback chair before him, for once missing his little cane's support.

Fleur offered a lopsided smile, watching Steve soak up the chamber. The books, the candles, the self-pouring pot of tea and the spoon slowly circling within the cup. Why hadn't he ever thought of that enchantment? The freshly baked muffins made his stomach growl. The sweet, warm scent of them flooded him with, what, comfort? What a strange feeling in a new place such as this.

"Steve?"

She stepped forward tentatively, a glittering trail swirling from her fingertips. As she wiggled those fine white digits, the misty flecks slowly settled into a shape between them. It was long, thin, and taller than herself.

Offering it to him, he took the magic offering. It solidified with his touch – a tall, wizened, wooden staff. A proper wizard's staff.

A glittering, light blue sapphire sat snugly in the burled wood at the tip, reflecting the teary constitution of his widened eyes. The staff took his weight, the constant pain in his ankle instantly forgotten.

"Steve?" Fleur tried again.

"Is this ..." A dream? Whoever she was, one thing was for sure –

Fleur was saving him from the nightmare of his life.

Steve the beardless wizard.

Gyn's younger, infirmed brother.

Father's greatest disappointment.

She read it all on his hairless face, or in his mind (perhaps she was telepathic? He'd be sure to find out soon).

Fleur smiled, moving to scoop up the full cup of tea on the table. The swirling spoon immediately stopped, the magical teapot's pouring mid-stream freezing instantly.

Fixing her gaze to his, she said warmly, cupping his soft cheek, "Welcome home."

Laura Honeysett

Laura Honeysett immersed herself in stories growing up and always dreamed of becoming a storyteller. Now as a loving mother of two active boys and passionate speech pathologist, Laura uses story in her everyday life, from teaching communication and literacy skills to compassionately supporting tricky behaviours and childhood development through story teaching.

YOU

by Laura Honeysett

"You're so dramatic."

"You're embarrassing me."

"You just don't fit in anywhere ..."

"You're like the ugly duckling."

You're not enough.

Their words.

Mine if I let them in ... when I let them in.

Like a photograph, I'm not really there at all

But trapped in time.

Surges of pain pulse through my body as my lower limbs are submerged in a murky sea.

Within moments bright flashes of red and blue blink towards me.

I'm transported to a land of bland, empty white.

Sterile.

Disconnected.

I am not safe here.

I obey.

I comply ... just as I was trained to do.

Choosing their words over my own, I ignore every natural instinct within my body.

The pain intensifies and surges through my body pushing me beyond my limits.

Sweat.

Shake.

Scream.

Push.

You.

Suddenly I am awake.

All at once I AM enough ... perhaps I always have been.

THEN, YOU.

by Laura Honeysett

I'm asleep but I hear you.

It's in these moments I actually hear you the most.

Loudly

You talk to me,

Tell me your coming.

"Just us," you say.

We are going to meet in the lounge room.

It will be late,

Dark,

And just us:

Your brother, you and me.

Sensations hit and I call for support.

Your Aunty and ambulance are on their way.

They talk.

"We have to go."

"Stand up."

"Move over there."

I block out the noise and listen within:

To you.

I surrender to my body.

It knows what to do,

In a state of flow.

I am safe,

Comfortable

And with your brother by my side,

You come

Just as you said you would.

When I share our story, we are asked:

"Was it a dream?"

"A reality?"

Well, perhaps it was both.

Family Manifest

by Laura Honeysett

I stand at the kitchen sink washing the dishes:

The usual routine.

A moment to catch my breath.

A moment to breathe.

Softening,

I close my eyes.

Two beautiful ,cheerful boys

Play in the garden we created together.

They talk to bugs,

Climb trees,

Plant seeds,

And nurture the land around us.

I join them.

A new figure joins in too.

My children and I enjoy their presence.

They build upon our joy

And live an intentional life.

Together we build, create and cook.

With full contented bellies, we

Journey to mysterious lands

Then pause to laze in the grass,

Searching for messages within the clouds.

My eyes open.

I see

My dream.

Our reality.

Woolvatoo

by Laura Honeysett

Lenny was one of those kids with a lively imagination. He could create cities out of fallen leaves, trampolines out of elastic bands and volcanoes out of tofu … yet he wasn't a big fan of his mum's "speciality" tofu casserole.

One morning, when Lenny was staying at his dad's house, he awoke with his most magical creation yet – Woolvatoo. Lenny rushed upstairs to where his dad was sleeping and began pounding on the bedroom door. Dad leaped out of bed startled.

"What's happened? Are you okay?" Dad said between short, sharp breaths.

Lenny paused and looked his Dad in the eye very seriously.

"Dad, I need to introduce you to someone. Now don't be scared, although he is big and rather shaggy he is also extremely kind and well tempered."

Dad looked at Lenny, confused as he gestured towards an empty space where the sun lit up specks of dust beside him. Lenny's face was now beaming, Dad's … was not.

"Quit dreamin' and go back to bed," grumbled Dad throwing the covers over his head as he slouched back into bed himself.

Lenny was confused. Why wouldn't Dad want to be friends with

Woolvatoo? He was only the coolest creature that ever existed! Lenny shrugged and leaped downstairs where he proceeded to make Woolvatoo a nutritious breakfast of sardine, sausage and baked bean tacos. Lenny and Woolvatoo played all day whilst Dad worked on his laptop, looking up every now and then with concern spread across his face as Lenny gave the air hugs, high fives and other *less familiar* gestures.

When the afternoon came, Mum arrived and Lenny jumped into her arms at full speed. Somehow, Mum managed to catch Lenny with only a little side stumble. The pair did a wacky kind of *throw your hands in the air dance* that they invented when Lenny was only three years old. Lenny gave Dad a *see ya later* cuddle, grabbed his bag and jumped into the car.

"Guess what's for dinner tonight LenMan!" said Mum in her enthusiastic *I'm so cool* voice.

Lenny shrugged. "Not tofu casserole is it?"

Mum laughed. "Not tonight. Instead, I was thinking veggie burgers and homemade chips."

Lenny sighed as they drove past a supermarket. "Woolvatoo really likes sausages, Mum ..."

Mum paused, confused and glanced in the car mirror.

In the back seat, she saw Lenny sitting solemnly, stroking Woolvatoo. With a smile, Mum put on the indicator and turned the car around.

"In that case we better make a pit stop and pick up some sausages on the way. What else does Woolvatoo like?"

"Oh, just the usual ... pretzels, popcorn and of course, frozen berries," said Lenny, livening up.

"Of course," Mum said. "The usual."

During dinner that night, Lenny told Mum all about Woolvatoo's crazy adventures. The three had a joyous time building blanket forts together and engaging in a *less than civil* pillow fight, before telling bedtime stories and cosying up for cuddles in the fort as music lulled them all to sleep.

The rest of that week seemed to speed by as Woolvatoo seamlessly became part of the family. Joining in with all of Lenny's home-school activities and endless adventures to the local library, beach, skate park and bush track. The only minor hiccup was when they met a snake on the bush track and Woolvatoo jumped five feet into the air before bouncing around like an electric pogo stick. Mum and Lenny had to add in an evening lesson around snakes that night, complimented by a very professional and informative toilet roll puppet show.

Lenny spent Saturday morning slowly packing his bags ready for Dad's house. Mum hovered in the doorway noticing the sad expression on Lenny's face.

"Woolvatoo will need more than one cuddly toy ... don't you think?" said Mum with a soft smile.

"Woolvatoo can't come to Dad's," replied Lenny. "Dad doesn't believe in him and doesn't like me *making up silly stories.* He says I'm *just dreamin'.*"

Mum paused for a moment, then sat on the bed next to Lenny. "Hmmm, have you ever heard the tale about the prickly giggle spider who lost his legs all in one day? Or the mouse who won one thousand eyes in a contest only to need glasses for all of them?"

"No!" Lenny laughed, climbing onto Mum's lap.

"Well I have, and let me tell you each one of those stories is ridiculous! I am telling you they are the silliest stories I have ever heard! But, they are also fun. I think everyone could use a bit more joy in their life, don't you?" Mum asked with a wink.

Lenny sat deep in thought for a moment then with widening eyes said excitedly, "Mum, I think I have an idea on how to get Dad to *see* Woolvatoo like I do ... but I'm going to need your help."

"Do you happen to also need some rags, the sewing machine, flour, scrap paper and food colouring?"

Lenny gave an enthusiastic nod before briskly setting to work on his plan.

That afternoon when Dad arrived to the usual pick up spot, he saw Lenny playing on the playground all by himself.

"Where's your Mum?" asked Dad, surprised that Lenny would have been left at the park on his own.

"Don't worry, I'm not alone," said Lenny with a cheeky smile and a head nod towards the nearby trees.

Just then Mum, dressed as Woolvatoo, jumped down from a tree and bounded towards the pair in her most convincing Woolvatoo performance. Dad couldn't help but laugh and ruffled his hands through Lenny's hair, amused.

"Well Lenny, it looks like Woolvatoo is real after all!" said Dad.

"Well kind of," replied Lenny, "but it doesn't really matter either way does it? Woolvatoo just reminds us to dream and to enjoy the moment."

"You know what Len, I think I wouldn't mind having Woolvatoo around after all!" Dad said in a thoughtful tone.

Lenny gave Mum an approving grin then turned back to Dad with a satisfied look.

"Seems, you're *just dreamin'* now too Dad!"

Jessica Giblin Jobson

Living on the sunny Central Coast, Jessica Giblin Jobson has always had a passion for writing, with many hours spent reading and creating her own stories. Her daughter, Amelia, has become the inspiration for her writing, creating a whole new realm of imagination to share with her. When she's not writing, Jessica enjoys time at the beach with her family, watercolour painting, and music.

Amelia's Dreams

by Jessica Giblin Jobson

Sometimes when I fall asleep,
tucked safely in my bed,
Images of scary things,
like tornadoes fill my head.

Sometimes it's volcanoes,
dinosaurs and spiders too,
But then I wake up Mummy,
she knows just what to do.

We talk about the happy things,
princesses and fairies,
From here my dreams are happy,
with nothing that is hairy.

We talk about the fun we'll have,
painting drawing too,
Maybe I will dream about
the monkeys at the zoo.

The adventures in dreams are endless,
so many routes to take,
Maybe there will be turtles,
swimming quietly in a lake.

Maybe I'll feed a kangaroo,
or with the mermaids swim,
I might fly up in the sky,
adventures on a whim.

I know that I am safe now,
a dream is my creation.
It's all about what I think up
in my imagination.

So now I can sleep soundly,
until the sun will rise,
I know I'll dream of wondrous things,
I can't wait to close my eyes.

Wen Gibson

Wen Gibson, author of the powerful and empowering memoir, *Stammering Against Truth*, has given us a heartfelt story of what it's like to dream. She followed her dreams, travelling the world on a bicycle, settling in Scotland, then returning to the Central Coast where she is passionate about her work as a counsellor. At the core of her life is kindness.

Amelia Moptop

by Wen Gibson

Amelia Moptop liked to flop around all day. She flopped on the sofa in the lounge room before school, then flopped on her chair in the classroom. She flopped on her bed when she came home, exhausted from having to think all day. But best of all, she flopped on the floor in front of the television. This was her favourite flopping place, especially when she was upset.

At least once a week her mum confiscated her phone and she was banned from calling her friends. Her mum would put her phone in the special drawer with the lock. It hurt. She liked to flop when she was upset. It helped her feel less lost and alone.

"Amelia, you know you have to do your homework first. You can't be texting or calling your friends all afternoon. You've only just got back from school!"

"Oh, Mum, I forgot to tell them something ... please, can I have my phone back?"

"No. Do your homework. You can have it back tomorrow."

"I've done my homework. It was easy. Can I watch Young Sheldon?"

"Okay, but then you need to play with your sister."

Amelia turned on the television and flicked through the channels to find her favourite show. Then she flopped back on the carpet to watch what Young Sheldon was up to that day.

Her mother said, "Amelia, sit up straight."

But Amelia just flopped some more and said, "I've got floppy bones, Mum."

Amelia was tired of people telling her what to do. Everybody always had an opinion of how she should be. But what about her? With all their voices in her head, she couldn't hear her own.

Her teacher had said to her that morning, "Amelia, stand up straight." But Amelia just flopped some more against the classroom wall.

She said, "I've got floppy muscles, Miss."

They didn't understand. Flopping was useful. It let her sink into herself. She felt warm and fuzzy inside when she flopped. It stopped her getting worried and anxious and feeling like she was always doing it wrong. Nobody knew how important it was to flop. She could curl up with herself, like a worm or a caterpillar. Last week, she'd found a little green caterpillar crawling on the basil plant on the veranda. Her mum had asked her to pick some leaves for the tomato sauce. Amelia had carefully prised the tiny caterpillar off the leaf and placed it in her hand. It had curled up into a tight circle.

That's just like me, Amelia had thought, all tucked up safe and dreamy. She imagined the sun shining down through the leaves of the eucalypt tree, warming her back, and the soft breeze against her skin. She loved daydreaming when she was flopped up close.

She wondered if caterpillars dream too. Did they dream of turning into butterflies? It was easy for them. They knew what they were going to be. What was she going to turn into? Oh no. It was too scary. Better to flop and forget about it. Flopping was soothing.

All her friends at school knew what they wanted to do. They all had a passion of some sort. Of how they wanted to be all grown up and at university. Amelia didn't have a clue. It scared her.

Amelia's thoughts were interrupted by her grandmother calling out from the screen door at the front of the house.

"Amelia! It's me. Let me in. My hands are full of shopping."

Amelia opened the door and stood to one side to let her grandmother pass. In a stern voice, her grandmother reprimanded Amelia.

"Amelia, how many times do I have to tell you? Walk with your head up straight. You're all over the place."

But Amelia purposely flopped over some more and said, "I've got a floppy head, Grandma."

Why did nobody understand?

They didn't know how good it felt to flop. It felt right. Somehow, Amelia knew how to listen to herself when she flopped over. She knew what her heart wanted. It talked to her. When she was forced to stand up straight, all she heard was the other person. When she had to stand up tall, she couldn't find herself.

She didn't know what she felt.

She needed to flop.

One day, when Amelia was flopping in her favourite place in front of the TV, she realised her program wasn't on. She quickly flicked through again just to be sure Young Sheldon wasn't somewhere else. She heard the announcer say, "The Australian Open Tennis Tournament is being televised live from Melbourne."

Oh dear, Amelia thought, what am I going to do? Amelia felt sorry for herself and flopped further in front of the TV. She felt lonely. No one wanted to flop with her. It was a beautiful sunny day outside, and her little sister was soaring higher and higher on the swing, squealing her delight with each push of her legs. Her little brother was shoving a tractor through the sand in the sandpit, making engine noises, and all her friends were at the beach.

Suddenly, Amelia's attention was caught. She stared at the television. The world's number one women's tennis player, Iga Swiatek, had stepped onto the court.

Amelia was mesmerised.

This woman looked like her. Same quiet face and slender form. She didn't look muscley like her opponent, Sabalenka, who stood up fiercely straight. She didn't grunt or push or fist pump. Iga looked purposeful and determined. Amelia liked it. It called to her and her floppy heart. Something inside her woke up. She sat up.

Amelia watched Iga run from one side of the tennis court to the other, chasing every ball. She watched as Iga hit the balls back hard and fast. Amelia whooped out loud when Iga hit an overhead smash and it veered into the back corner of the court, winning the final point of the game.

A strange feeling came over Amelia Moptop. Her heart had started beating, almost like it was talking to her from her chest. It was almost wild with excitement. It was saying to Amelia, *Amelia, we can do that too. We can hit a ball. It looks like fun.*

She and her heart had woken up. Her heart said again, *Amelia, let's try it. You know all those daydreams we've had together underneath the tree? Or when we flopped on the sofa? Those dreams we had when we imagined ourselves moving and growing and feeling strong and free. Well, this is it. We can do this together. Do you want to give it a go?*

Her heart wanted her to move. It prodded her.

She sat up and stretched. She knew.

Yes. She felt it.

It felt right to stand up.

She stood up and reached up high. It felt good to expand.

She wanted to walk with her head proud and tall.

We can do this together, her heart murmured again, encouraging her. *Come on you, it's time to let our dreams come alive.*

Amelia practiced walking around the room swinging her right arm as if hitting a tennis ball. She imagined the thud of the shot and how it would shoot across the net. Suddenly, it wasn't enough. She wanted a tennis racquet like Iga. She wanted to feel it in her hand. She wanted to hit a ball hard and fast. She wanted to run. Amelia

Moptop felt alive. She felt electric.

Feeling wonderful, she didn't want to flop in front of the television anymore. Her floppy heart was yelling like the crowd on the TV.

"Amelia Moptop steps onto centre court," her heart was commentating, cheering her on.

Amelia didn't feel floppy at all. Her floppiness had metamorphosed just like a caterpillar. She was turning into a butterfly who wanted to fly. Instead, she ran into the kitchen and shouted,

"Please Mum, can I play tennis?"

Brendan Gulson

After dabbling with short stories and poetry in his younger years, Brendan Gulson really found his creative feet upon moving to the country in 2014. Brendan's writing and artwork is inspired by a deep-seated connection with the landscape and an ongoing interest in history and mysticism. He is currently wondering where all the Bohemians have gone.

In Love with the Verdant Vale

by Brendan Gulson

Prelude:
I'm half-way through writing a tale, sitting on my deck, lost in the fantasy of the story. Trying to engage the mind of a new friend with the fecundity of my imagination. The tale is a highly-corrupted version of 'The Epic of Saint Brendan'. My namesake, and possibly my character in the faery tale of life – a mad monk, searching and striving …

An excerpt:
The protagonists have just visited the Isle of Seals. A new island is in view, and the writer is describing the motivations of the three voyagers:

And the supposed hero of the tale? Well …

In a way, you've got to wonder what he's doing in a travel story – he's not particularly fond of travel.

"There is more to explore in my mind," he says.

But the truth is he does a lot of reading, and thinking, and writing. And the imagination be a powerful thing indeed.

And here lies one of the glittering gems of human existence on Earth – imagining something to be; dreaming; whether asleep or awake; is, for a while at least, as real, and valid, as the rest of life.

And the wonderful thing about dreams, (aspirations? fantasies?) is that, with enough determination, courage and luck, they can be made solid.

There is a photo of me when I was around six years of age, sitting on the front porch, surrounded by my furry friends – teddy bears and the like. Lost in that beautiful world of the young child's imagination, I'm not sure that dreams featured much in the landscape.

Jump forward eight years. In the days when the internet didn't exist, and computer games caused less obsession, my neighbour, Pat, and I would kick a footy to each other on the suburban street where we lived.

In the classic naïve way of the young and inexperienced, we would dream of the future. In our youthful fantasies, we had bought a big country property, and lived either end of it.

Two years later, and I had undergone a transformation of consciousness. Sparked off by the convictions of a passionate geography teacher, I had rapidly developed a world view that saw contemporary Western culture and it's material trappings as an object of contempt. I had been radicalised.

These feelings didn't go away. They became stronger, to the point of where I felt compelled to distance myself from mainstream society, to seek an alternative. And the place I had heard of, where people sought a different way of living?

Nimbin.

So, fresh from high school and middle-class suburbia, I took myself off to the Far North Coast. I can't quite recall where I first came across ideas of self-sufficiency, but I remember that the initial place I stayed had stacks of *Earth Garden* and *Grass Roots* magazines. My young head was filled with idealistic dreams.

At the next place I stayed, with no real idea of what I was doing, and no guidance, I tried growing my own vegetables. And failed to produce much more than a spindly bok choy or two.

The ramshackle cabin I shared with a much older housemate had an outdoor loo, no proper running water, and snakes used to poke their heads through holes in the unfinished ceiling.

It was further south, in another hippie enclave outside of Bowraville, that I came across a version of Paradise. A verdant valley surrounded by tree-covered hills with a pure freshwater stream running out of the rainforest. Content cattle wandering in lush paddocks, vegetable gardens, stands of giant bamboo, a native nursery, huge dome-shaped Red Cedars. A magical and inspiring landscape.

Not long afterwards, I returned to the city and somehow got stuck there. Then the responsibilities of adulthood came tumbling down upon me, and I found myself back in suburbia, with young children, a mortgage, and a business to run. Overwhelmed by this weight of dutiful chores, my dreams of an Arcadian idyll were put firmly on hold. Life had become a day-to-day reality of encumbrance.

But, look a little closer. See how the dreamer keeps his fantasy alive through the imagination? Where do most of the bedtime stories for his girls take place? In the countryside. In forests and verdant vales. In places of a slower pace, where Magic flits around the edges, like a cheeky sprite.

Scoot ahead six years. The marriage has broken down. Suddenly, out of the gloom of a train wreck, the old dream of a place in the country emerges ...

The dream is within reach!

Acreage, but not too distant from the ex-wife's.

It's easy now, of course, to find real estate. Everything at one's fingertips, thanks to the Almighty Internet.

Oh, this one looks good. It looks perfect. Accompanied by my mum and dad, we check out it out.

We drive into the property. Up, down, around, into a hidden valley. On an impulse, I stop the vehicle. Jump out and pry my fingers into the soil.

Loam!

Black Gold.

The Holy Grail.

A cabin needing work. A verdant vale surrounded by tree-clothed hills. Top of the catchment. End of the road. Freshwater creek streaming out of the rainforest. Red Cedars.

Looks like the Dream has come true...

Carlyn Smith

Carlyn Smith is a young emerging author with a passion for storytelling and mental advocacy. Carlyn's work blends traditional narratives with modern concerns. *Mother Koala* is centered around the threatened wildlife caused by dry bushfires in Australia. Through vivid storytelling, Carlyn seeks to raise awareness about the environmental challenges affecting Australian wildlife.

Mother Koala

by Carlyn Smith

A grey cloud of fluff hidden up within the trees;
is it an animal or the gazing silhouette of the Southern Cross?

The lengthy scars that inbred into the gumtree branches
seeps at the seams and our friend sits there in silence.

An orange and gold blaze ignites the vermillion oak.
The dried up eucalyptus forest slowly starts to burn as the
crickets' creek in agony.

As acres of heavenly saplings fall into blistering ashes,
the rising heat kindles the smokey chlamydic coat.

Joeys of one panic in the pouch of Mother as
their bodies start sweltering in the raging red flames.

Mother grips the weak bough and descends down the tree,
her babies are heavy and it's difficult to move fast.

She tries to flee while her joeys convey but somehow
the rapid fires are faster, breathing is minimal and mothers bones
ache.

"If I don't risk them, then there will be eventually none of us left."

Bronwyn Boehm

Now living on NSW's beautiful north coast, Bronwyn Boehm has enjoyed several analytical careers in city and regional Australia, while writing throughout. Bronwyn is resurrecting her creative soul through fiction as her true passion lies in writing short stories. Her quest is to immortalise the Australian psyche at its most basic and beautiful through quirky yet poignant tales.

Myth Understood

by Bronwyn Boehm

"Beer?"

Water lapped the myriad moss-rimmed stones edging the creek. Low slow kook-kooks swelled to riotous cackles through sighing treetops.

"Yeah."

Both firm believers in doing and saying the barest minimum, Matty kicked a tinnie across to Josh. A triggering pfft of welling froth ensued with synchronised slurping, stretching and scratching. The brothers' hectic day softened to a close.

Matty pulled out his phone.

"Leave it," Josh said, "purpose of this weekend, wasn't it?"

Matty ignored him.

Born in the same year, they were almost twins. Same dark hair and eyes, same classes in school, same sports teams, same job. And like actual twins, they simultaneously liked and loathed their familiarity – the bonus having a mate who knows you inside-out versus him pre-empting your every move. Regardless, they always worked things out and remained close. Until recently.

Their trip into the wild mountains was their mother's idea.

No internet, just them.

"You boys need to get sorted, breathe in the magic there." She persisted, and eventually they agreed. Things were way out of hand.

Matty met Hannah, the wild redhead with teal green eyes and a smile that outshone footy-field floodlights. And Josh moved in on her. She liked them both: Matty the 'smart, silent one with the soulful eyes'; and Josh the 'funny, sunny one with the come-hither grin'.

She was tearing them apart.

The clichéd love triangle went viral. Excruciating comments, unending awkward images, thousands of scornful followers. Hannah lapped up the attention while the world plagued and ridiculed the brothers. Yet both remained smitten. Game on.

"No coverage." Matty pocketed his phone. "Might try up on the ridge tomorrow."

"Going for a leak." Josh strode across the clearing.

Sparks spiralled up from the fire's cobalt-streaked orange spears, vibrant and mesmerising. Matty sighed, kicked ashes, slapped mozzies, downed a beer, opened another.

"You okay, mate?"

No answer.

He walked to the edge of the clearing and let rip an ear-splitting whistle.

A low growl rumbled behind him. Josh sprung out.

"Haha, very funny."

"No, it's huge!" Josh was wide-eyed and panting.

"Not falling for …" Matty turned and instantly froze.

Looming beside the tent, as if from an old black-and-white horror movie, the shadowy form of a gigantic ape-man spat and snarled, teeth glinting in the flickering firelight. It lumbered around the campsite, snapping branches and crushing tins, hairy boulder-fists swaying low.

Matty stood rooted to the spot gaping. Summoning a beer-fuelled bravado, Josh lunged towards the fire and grabbed a burning stick. The creature roared and rose up to its impressive height. But committed to the moment, Josh lurched forward screaming and flaying cinders in crazy swipes.

"Stop! You'll set fire to the tent, y'idiot!"

Galvanised into action, Matty scooped up their dinner's leftovers and hurled them into the bush.

The thing howled and thundered off after the scraps into the underbrush. Chests heaving, the brothers stood motionless, scanning the shadows for movement.

"A yowie! Never would've believed … aagh!" Josh flung the smoking branch away and shook his smarting hand.

Matty dragged out his sleeping bag and settled into his camp chair near the fire, cradling an axe. "Sleeping out tonight."

Josh soon followed suit.

Dawn's lemon light crept across craggy sentinel ridges. Raucous kookaburras roused the two cocoons sprawling on tilting chairs. Two heads emerged twisting stiff-neck cracks. Wide yawns and foul farts followed.

"You okay?"

"Still here."

The clearing resembled a demolition site. Throughout the night, they scrambled for fire sticks, rocks, anything to deter marauding yowies, each time discovering a troupe of small nocturnal marsupials about as dangerous as kittens.

They started cleaning up. Whether on the footy field, cricket pitch or building site, they always functioned as one. A well-oiled machine. Naturally, conversation was mostly pointless.

"Think we imagined that gross thing? We'd had a few." Matty rubbed his scalp in a futile attempt to relieve its throb.

Josh tossed coffee dregs hissing into the fire. "I'd swear it was real."

Hours later they crested a ridge and squinted back down into the campsite, patches visible through the shifting canopy.

Josh thumped Matty's arm. "Still scared, ya wuss?"

Matty swigged on his water bottle and returned a punch. "You? Hopping around last night like Tinkerbell whose tutu's on fire."

"Ha! Thought you wet your pants, staring like a zombie."

Matty scrutinised the next valley. "A waterhole." He set off towards a dense patch of vegetation, glowing verdant in the grey-green gorge. "Better watch out for yowies Tinkers. And dropbears."

Hesitant cicada chirps accelerated to deafening screeches as the brothers emerged hot and sweating onto an overhanging rock. Below them, a wide pool of deep moss-green water undulated in the still air, fed by a trickling fern-dipped stream. Josh pulled off his boots and shirt.

"Hang on." Matty gazed around.

"Ya wuss!" Josh stripped naked and dashed forward, grabbed his knees mid-air and with an almighty splash landed in the pool, bare bum first.

Head shaking and still spooked, Matty peered over the edge.

Metres from Josh's bobbing body, a murky underwater shadow mushroomed and burped concentric ripples that began vying with the churns from his brother's antics. The ominous swelling rings released a putrid stench that wafted up the ravine. Suddenly, a hideous bulldog-like skull breached the centre. Matty stiffened. A thick black neck and slick muscled torso surged up.

"Hey! Josh!"

The creature's head swung upwards at the sound of Matty's yell. Its gaping crimson sabre-toothed maw unleashed a spine-chilling scream.

Matty's glance swept to his pale submerged brother, zig-zagging unsuspecting. Wrenching off boots, he sprang off the rock wide.

The grotesque tusked head roared. Enormous knife-clawed limbs writhed the surface. The monster rose up and out, thrashing towards Josh.

Matty plunged deep, wrenching at Josh in the algae-roiled depths, yanking, kicking frantically. Angry bubbles bloomed over Josh's face.

Surfacing, Josh spluttered, gasping.

Matty clamped an arm under his chin and, not daring to look back, side-stroked Josh ashore.

"Geez Matty!" Josh shook the water from his ears and hair. "What ...?"

"Look!" Matty pointed back at the bizarre water creature.

Aghast, Josh stared as the ferocious grimacing head shrieked a final threat. It snarled rancid froth as its massive slimy shoulders slid back into the roiling abyss. Not until the disgusting foam had completely dissipated did either brother relax.

"What the hell was that?"

"Dunno." Hands on hips, Matty scanned the ravine again. "Something strange is going on in these mountains."

"No kidding."

"Dropbears are a joke, sure, but that yowie last night and now this thing? Dreamtime myths?"

"Nah, myths are the crap parents use to keep kids in line." Josh shivered. "That thing was real."

Matty climbed back up and found his phone. "Good. Two bars." He frowned. "Appears this water monster is a bunyip. And yep, last night's was a yowie."

"Not possible," Josh was suddenly furious. "They're just monster stories. We're wide awake, not dreaming all this. And we both saw them. And heard them."

"And smelt them. Like Mum said, weird stuff happens up here." Matty swiped to another screen and scowled.

Josh skipped stones over the edge. "What's she posted today?"

"More of the same."

Silent and frowning, they dried off and headed back.

Basking snakes slithered off the track. Flashing white cockatoo flecks soared along far shimmering ridges, their screeches drifting through the pulsating heat as the brothers descended.

"Umm, thanks for saving me." Josh huffed and paused for a drink under the shade of a mountain ash. Languid goannas sauntered at an arrogant distance, blue forked tongues darting.

"Yeah, me too. For last night."

An inquisitive wallaby curtsied behind blossom-dusted wattles, one ear riffling flies, the other cocked.

"We're still tight, you and me, yeah?"

"Guess so." Josh hunched down beside him, head low, lips barely moving. "Think that's why Mum suggested this weekend."

"Yeah." Matty thrummed a fist on his thigh. "Mum and her mystical view on life. Said the air up here's different. Peaceful. Therapeutic."

Josh's feeble scoff was unconvincing. Thoughts floated above them, as elusive as the channels of hot air quivering the pungent gum leaves there. He broke the silence.

"Hannah is ..." his voice was a rusty knife, stabbing ribs.

"... playing us," Matty finished the treacherous thought. "It's all just fun and fame for her. At our expense."

"She doesn't understand us, the weird together us."

"And she's jealous of our bond. So 'divide and conquer'."

The rusty knife twisted deep in painful harmony.

Later, around the campfire they settled again with beers in hand. Matty squinted up through the trembling treetops to a navy star-speckled sky.

"So, those crazy monsters," Josh said. "Whatever they're called ... They were real."

"Yeah, real. To us." Matty dragged his eyes back to face his brother square-on. "We're so tight that everything we hear, see, even everything we do is the same."

"Rubbish! We imagined all that? Then why attack us?"

"Honestly, you're thick sometimes. It's as if we're attacking each other."

"But we saved each other."

"Exactly. Healing, Mum said."

Dorothy Swoope

Dorothy Swoope is a widely published, award-winning writer. Her publications include The Touch of a Word, Moments of Distraction and her childhood memoir Wait 'til Your Father Gets Home! She resides on the South Coast of New South Wales.

Prescient

by Dorothy Swoope

It was a dream I had in Oregon

walking on a golden beach

beside a golden man

each of us leading a horse

like something out of *Clan of the Cave Bear*

though I hadn't read it yet.

Next morning I remembered my dream

sharing it with my friend, Marcie

in the green mossy woods

with a whisper of the sea to seal our secrets.

Years later living in Australia

the dream rebloomed in full-bodied déjà vu

as I stitched ornamental beadwork to my hessian saddlebag

in preparation for a horse trek up the coast with my friend

walking on a golden beach

with a golden man

each of us leading a horse.

It was a dream I had in Oregon.

Glofernwolfe

Glofernwolfe is a writer and a self-taught artist whose work blends futuristic dystopia with grounded realism. Growing up in India, he travelled widely—from the chaotic pulse of industrial metropolises like Mumbai to the majestic stillness of the snowy Himalayas. These contrasting landscapes reflect strongly in the worlds he builds in his writing and art.

Terror Kitchen

by Glofernwolfe

Amma. It's this place, or what, I don't know. Sometimes I feel like things are real. But I know they're not.

Do you remember telling me: there are times when we see our destiny in our dreams? It's alright if you don't remember. I should never have left home. I don't know when I can come back – all I can do is write to you whenever I get the chance.

It's the same job, Amma. Travelling to Petersham every morning. Then coming back late in the evening; there's no time to cook dinner, so it's American food every night. They call it "Maccas" here; so funny their words are.

You know my journeys are lonely; two hours just sitting and staring at the vapid Australian outback. Sometimes I see kangaroos, otherwise it's only cockatoos that interest me.

It's been raining all week. I like it when the skies are blue though. The clouds are much bigger and fluffier here.

Today I met someone on the train. This tall, brawny girl sat across from me. Her physiognomy was very abstruse, like most people here. Everyone is a mix of cultures, except me.

"Where ya headed, fam?" she asked, so I just said I'm going to work at Terror Kitchen. That's what me and the boys call it now, Amma.

The "soop" is a real nightmare for all of us. I'll tell you why later.

"What brings you to Gadigal Country, then?" She was not insolent, only curious, I think.

I liked her green-blue eyes, so rare in our country. Her skin was tanned, like milk chocolate, but it looked golden when the sunlight caressed her face. What looked peculiar was that her nylon jacket was the same colour as her red-brown hair that she tied in two braids. But of course, I didn't comment.

"Work," I said. "I've been here only for a year or so."

"Righto." Now, I knew she grew up here. "My name's Juli. The Sham's our area, boy. My mob's got the place running nice and happy. Anyone give you trouble, you call my name. Got it?"

I only nodded, Amma. I don't like getting into gang business. So many reports I see on TikTok and on the news – everyday someone or the other gets into trouble. But crime is not so bad here. It's peaceful as far as I've seen.

The downpour was so heavy that rainwater began collecting inside our cabin. It even started flooding; so clear the water was that I could see my face reflected on the steel tread plates. She went, then, that girl – Juli. And I got off at Petersham.

I reached Terror Kitchen early. I saw the boys avoiding the soop, and I realised why when I presented myself.

Her halitosis had worsened; I almost choked when she asked me for my bump-in time. She eyed me through her veil of unkempt blonde hair – her wrinkly pale skin twitched as she smirked when she looked at me up and down like a school principal.

What scared me most, was her eyes. It was opaline, like your pearl necklace, Amma. I only glanced, because I still cannot look people in the eyes.

She would never give me fryer duty again, not after yesterday's debacle. She told me to let the fries cook till she returned. She didn't come back for half-an-hour, Amma. She was watching the game. Then she blamed *me*!

She also made me throw out cold fries that were sitting on the edge of the bain marie for hours. What utter waste! The food industry is horrible, Amma! I wish I had taken up the job offer at Woolies.

But today was much worse. There were so many untoward customers with pet tarantulas and I had to serve them despite my fear of spiders. And I was in charge of the pizzas, and they were getting sold faster than we could make them. I kept away from the non-vegetarian ones, I promise.

There was so much commotion in the kitchen that at one point I slipped where one of the boys had spilled flour, and I was carrying a deep gastronorm tray full of pizza sauce. It was the middle of the game, Amma. Half-time!

Indecorous customers were climbing over the counter demanding cheese pizzas! I was covered in the hot sauce, and I felt like a spotlight was shining on me – burning my face, making me squint and frown.

She came then – the irascible soop. With her halitosis, and her slant, uncaring eyes. She smirked and shoved the boys aside.

"I've been waiting for this." She let out a harsh, derisive laugh. Her pink skin curved at the corner of her lips, almost imperceptibly.

And her lank blonde hair dripped with fryer oil.

I hugged myself, crumpling like paper, where I lay, ready to be chastised.

"Oi, touch him and you'll pay for it!" There was a voice behind her from where all the customers were peeking menacingly.

It was her, Amma. Juli. She came!

"Shut your eyes, boy," she told me. And I did.

But there was no sound of violence. No words, no screams.

All I heard was a recorded voice, "Next station, Petersham. Doors will open to the left. Please mind the gap between the door and the platform."

Is it true, Amma? Is our destiny sometimes manifested in our dreams?

Jorvn Jones

Jorvn's primary writing practice lays in poetry, but has encompassed essay and scriptwriting, blogging (social commentary/critique), and extending memoirs within online social context, in response to common themes in Jorvn's work. Jorvn has published in numerous publications (his full bio is available at the end of this anthology) including an obscure chapbook called *Vampire Tapeworms/Russian Tearooms*, which, if you can find a copy, you win a prize.

Ðream 1

by Jorvn Jones

(New Year's Eve)

Mon. 31/12/18

***

In a large backstage office area, seemingly mid-late 1970s era, swarming with the creative vivacious chattering of excited busy people of various genders, decked out in multi-coloured patterned mid-to-bright clothes and brown leather ensembles etcetera (could remind a bit of *The Muppet Show* backstage area, but different, and shot from multiple different angles), there is specific excitement surrounding me and what I am doing.

To one side, two long tall dusky-honey-blonde haired women (both with slightly grown out bobs, wavy) who remind somewhat of (well ... Janice in the Muppets ...) 70s era Barbra Streisand, or Carol Burnett in *Fresno* era, but aren't those (are their own people). They seem to keep a heraldic note of proceedings, as though watching both ways at the sharp edge of the stage, as it leads backstage. They are sort of in the dark, compared to the bright busy office space.

Amidst this commotion, a tiny Asian man (Filipino?) seems to be an authority figure there. He is dressed loudly, as though imitating the cover of *The Harder They Come*, but with a lot more mixed up styles, and clashes of colours and patterns (you're not sure where to focus), and customary brown leather (and plaids) stitched together to form stained glass window patterns of the various coloured leathers.

He does not seem out of place amidst the hubbub and razzledazzle, but he is clearly somehow in charge.

Not knowing where to look doesn't bother me, as I have my contract proffered in my hand. He takes me under his wing, hand on shoulder, and leads me through the tumultuous crowd, leaning in and talking conspiratorially, if somewhat leery. (The sort of leeriness common to 70s showbiz situations, given credence by the amount of people backstage.)

He has a silver satin soft cod-piece, and, as he takes me with his arm and clenches around my neck, I am surprised that the truss part is not as hard or as scaly as I had anticipated.

The two blonde women also keep their account of it, and their gazes seem more keen now.

I notice intensely that the backstage lights are very bright, electric and yellow. Quickly enough, just when it seems about he will finish speaking, we are suddenly interrupted by a flash of bright light. We turn to the side in the shock of surprise.

-end-

Ðream 3

by Jorvn Jones

(Early morn. Midday-ish)

Thurs. 22/02/18

Taurus Moon.

no CPAP Mask (possible under weather)

rather long & elaborate dream (at about 11hrs sleep,
no CPAP Machine on ...)

***

Started at that house in London, a cottage in a field behind industrial lit city, at night, it is silent and alone. I have abandoned it but gone back. There is no occupant, but I am aware of trespassing. They may be there at some point, could it be any moment? The main floor is still, and occupied with their (her?) furniture, I don't pay it much attention, but scan it (from outside through the window) as though they may walk in at any moment.

I ascend into the attic space through a loose eave, where my bizarre and elaborate abandoned antiques I left behind are stored, in darkness. This sequence is repeated several times, but not the poaching/removal of them; but it is acknowledged, or encapsulated within the dream.

(Upon waking, I'm still not sure if that place ever did exist. Why such a vivid sense memory for an object of imagination? ...)

Cut to: He's building a rival building, light and airy, big high white ceilings, curving over, suggesting space. He is pensive, the hero, not quite an anti-hero, but with the stubble and weathered skin of an 80s action hero in motion pictures. Kind of generic, but distinctive enough in focus that you somehow know he is in charge, though he doesn't take the lead over specific actions. His presence is there, as though you are viewing the scenario through his lens.

It's obviously his place, like at a party where you meet an unassuming average nobody, then at the end of your conversation, he casually says, "It's mine."

He is not pictured throughout, but you use his eyes.

His large atrium style rooms are soon taken over by a mass exodus from outside. They could be extras from a prison flick. Very athletic, they take on natural roles of assembly. There are amazing feats of athletic activity, a hive abuzz.

A recurring trope is an androgynous figure - Caucasian, with cropped spiky/sandy hair, not unlike Amanda Bearse, but probably not her. She is doing a stunning, cracking gymnastics routine in the foreground, on a trapeze swinging from invisible rafters in the aerodrome atrium curvature of the domed roof, her body snapping to attention and back, like a Swiss Army Knife flicking out, to and fro ~ SNAP! back SNAP! back SNAP! back ... etc ...

Our pensive hero seems somewhat overwhelmed by these masses

of people, and wanders around trying to organise them into workgroups. But stuff gets done regardless, there is nothing really to worry about.

It is quite an impressive centre. There is really no need to think about the rival building. But often he flashes back to the dark mysterious (Was it there?) London building, with its enigmatic cargo of rare precious antiques, like a marker, a clock looming, a bomb ticking.

This bright and airy rival building, with its mass of possible cons, is a busy buzzing hive of activity. Cut between the various scenarios ad infinitum until awake ... (slightly groggy ...)

-end-

Electrical Dreams

by Jorvn Jones

Sometimes a dream'll keep you from a crazy scene

other times'll push you right in

I got electrical storm dreams last night

like fireflies or moths batting at my eyes

sometimes all the concretes just like quicksand

dreams make you want to question the plan

in another dream again ...

is it good to smile 'cos it makes me feel Zen?

is that the sort of thing that breaks the trance?

or is it so pure and strong

that it with-

stands?

Ðrempt Fragment

by Jorvn Jones

Dreamt I was organising a horn section in a Victorian town, and would meet them at the church hall. Caught a lift there with some close woman confidante, and we drove through the dark night alleys some shortcut the back way, pretty direct, crossing over lots of streets, with looming dark brick viaducts running alongside us on the left.

She had a trumpet, so, to while away the time on the drive, I began to play it, though the stopgap on the mouthpiece didn't matter, and I played an amusing panoply of combinations with the buttons, even finding new ones, which quite surprised even me, but I brushed it off and was nonchalant about it, but everyone was pretty lowkey.

We got to the place, and were staying in the hall next door, with her boyfriend, a dark brooding but fun man with flowing wild long black hair like an afro that had kept growing, and a dark bear like a five o'clock shadow that had kept going.

We had arrived sometime before his going to bed and he kept up with us throughout the rest of the night, sometimes coming and going. I was mainly concerned about the trumpet, but there were conversationals (this dream wasn't a talkie ...), all very dark in his rooms where he did stay.

The woman busied herself about the place, and when he did

disappear off somewhere, I went to a room at the back, which may have been toilet, and discovered there wasn't much to this place, it was just cluttered, and looked in the mirror, fingering the stopgap of the mouthpiece of the trumpet, but, before I could really look in the mirror (it was dark) he came back, and was fussing around me, like, *What are you doing back here?*, and so I decided to go outside, and, by now, people had started arriving in their cars on the lawn (it was set out like my old Sunday school, except his building was nothing like their hall, and we didn't make it into the church ...), so I spoke to an old girl I knew from art school, and was catching up with her in the back of her station wagon, across a long board laid horizontally between us like a table, with wares upon it.

This wasn't a talkie, but she was talking, and it was still night, in anticipation of something, like before a great big performance or something.

She was white, and she did most of the talking, and seemed quite happy and cheerful, despite her lank fringe, which she had fixed with blue hair dye. She had a blue plastic toy (like one might find in a lucky dip, such as had been pulled from a cereal box or some such ...) of a cowboy and his apprentice watching him swinging a lariat (or a lasso) pierced through her lip, and when I looked at it, I thought how much it reminded me of the Harpic blue colour of cleaning toilets, so, in my mind's eye, I flashed onto the bright white toilet bowl I pictured, streaked through & streaming in patterns with pristine Harpic blue liquid. I flashed on this maybe two or three times, while she was talking, unawares.

(This still wasn't a talkie.)

It was still dark, but well lit, on the lawn, where people were starting to gather. Some fancy women friends of hers, very arty and snooty and formal and professional seeming, but curious and friendly and not afraid, gathered at the rolled down back window of the station wagon where we were sitting, and began to talk to her.

I began to explore my trumpet, and became aware I couldn't get the silvery stopgap from the brassy gold of the mouthpiece, no matter what buttons I tried to push.

Suddenly, the lead chick of this posse of women, a mousy-but-not-mousy blonde chick with wiry circular John Lennon glasses and hair that she obviously didn't do anything with, but it didn't matter, kinda wild and untamed and free look, was sitting next to me on my left, further into the interior of the car, and I hadn't noticed her climb through. Staring boldly at the art school chick, talking earnestly.

The other chicks were still outside, gathered at the window, not making any commotion about how they weren't inside the station wagon.

It still wasn't a talkie, but we were involved in a conversation about the impending performance, or so it seemed.

The art school chick seemed nonchalant, happy enough to be talking with these strange people in her car, but with something held back, like some hidden knowledge, but it could have just been she was happy enough to be anywhere, could have been anywhere, so long as she was in her station wagon. Her smiling face became more social, like her words didn't matter, they were just chitter chatter.

I began to notice her blue doodad in her lip even more. It was still, and never swung. Her face seemed quite light.

Her friend opposite her was dressed in quite dark clothes, like, maybe a black turtleneck or something, very Art School Confidential, but her face was very round and light-skinned with the earnest wire-framed glasses, and her hair was messy dishwater blonde.

They kept talking earnestly and noiselessly.

Suddenly, the focus was upon my trumpet, and we all agreed it didn't matter about the stopgap, and I didn't know how to play the keys, 'cause when I pressed the buttons, magic happened and I played like it wasn't the devil's business.

To demonstrate, I tentatively placed my mouth around the silver stopgap, and we all realised at once that it didn't matter, and I could play beautifully, so I did a little virtuoso display, right there in the back of the station wagon, with the church looming darkly above with its spire.

And then we were talking frantically about the weird associations of keys and buttons I was using in unconventional and complex patterns, particularly the blonde one. She was going wild, and her hair was getting messier.

But it still wasn't a talkie.

And then I woke up.

[approx. 7 1/2 hrs]

Tara Jean

Tara Jean is an emerging author based in Brisbane. A proud Wiradjuri woman, she is connected to her Aboriginal heritage and celebrates her culture through storytelling. She loves teaching, psychology, stargazing and researching anything related to First Nations science.

The Rift

by Tara Jean

The heavy, thick air held a silence, broken only by the chirps of field bugs. Avery lay sprawled on her bed, arms stretched out, eyes fluttering shut with a mix of exhaustion and anticipation. In her haste for rest, she'd not even kicked off her grubby shoes, and instead, her feet dangled over the edge of the bed.

After a gruelling workday in the fields, there was nothing more Avery wanted than to fall into her dreams. But her dreams were not ordinary – they were a vivid, kaleidoscopic realm where the laws of reality seemed to dissolve into the extraordinary. A place where she could escape.

Avery had always been a lucid dreamer. From a young age, her nights were filled with adventures, strange encounters, and landscapes that shimmered with a surreal brilliance. Her dreams were her sanctuary, a place where she could escape the monotony of life as a field worker in this small, forgettable village.

By day, she harvested wheat and exchanged small talk with the other villagers; by night, she soared across skies painted in auroras, danced with starlit beings, and unravelled the mysteries of worlds that felt beyond comprehension. But her dreams came with a secret. One she ran from every day, praying the realm soldiers did not catch up with her.

Lately, something had shifted. Avery's dreams were becoming more persistent, more purposeful, as if carrying a message she couldn't quite grasp hold of. And this evening, as she surrendered to sleep, she had the feeling that something profound was waiting for her on the other side.

The transition into a dream state was seamless.

One moment
she was enveloped
by the humidity in her small room,
body slick with sweat, and the next, she was
standing in the middle of a vast desert under a violet sky.

The sand beneath her now bare feet sparkled like crushed gemstones, and the air was filled with the faint melody of an invisible orchestra. Squinting, Avery could see that off into the distance a lone figure stood, cloaked in robes that shimmered like liquid gold.

Avery approached cautiously. The figure turned to face her, revealing an ageless face with eyes that sparkled.

"Avery," the figure spoke. "You have been summoned."

"Summoned?" Avery repeated, her voice echoing strangely in the dreamscape. "By who?"

The figure extended a hand, palm upward, and a swirling orb of light appeared. Within it, images flickered: a forest ablaze, a river splitting into two paths, and a towering mountain crowned with storm clouds.

"The Dreaming is not merely an escape," the figure explained. "It is a bridge between realms, a place where destinies are woven. You have been chosen to traverse this bridge."

The figure's gaze softened. "Dreamers like you are rare, Avery. But you already know this. You possess the ability to shape the Dreaming and influence the waking world. But there is a tear in the fabric of dreams. If it is not mended, both realms will collapse."

Avery's heart raced. This was not the whimsical adventure she had expected. She knew she could dream wield, and had been running ever since she found out, ever since the soldiers found out, as she knew not how to control it.

"How do I fix it?"

"By facing the shadows that dwell within you and within the Dreaming," the figure said. "The journey will be perilous, but you will not be alone."

As the figure spoke, the desert began to shift and shimmer, transforming into a dense forest bathed in silver light. Standing amidst the trees was a sleek, black panther with eyes like molten gold.

"He will guide you," the figure said before fading into a cascade of golden sparks.

The panther approached her with a fluid grace, its voice resonating in her mind. "I am Kye, the shadow of courage. To face the unknown, you must first confront fear."

Avery nodded, and together, they began their journey through the forest. The path was winding and narrow, with roots scattered across the path that seemed to writhe like serpents and shadows that whispered. At times, Avery felt the weight of doubt pressing down on her, but Kye's steady presence bolstered her resolve.

"I still don't understand why me?" she asked. Without looking at her, Kye flicked his long black tail, seemingly annoyed.

"All in good time, everything will become apparent."

As they ventured further, the forest gave way to a sprawling river, its waters dark and churning. Two bridges spanned its width: one old and rickety, the other gleaming and solid. Kye eyed Avery curiously. "Appearances can be deceiving. Which will you choose?"

Avery hesitated, her eyes darting between the two bridges. Logic urged her to choose the sturdy one, but a quiet intuition pulled her toward the rickety bridge. The bridge was familiar and reminded her of her past life, before the soldiers came. She took a deep breath and stepped onto the older bridge, its wooden planks creaking beneath her weight. To her relief, it held firm, and they crossed without incident.

"Well done," Kye said, his tone approving. "Trusting your instincts is key here in the Dreaming."

Once on the other side of the river, the landscape shifted again. They now stood at the base of the towering mountain Avery had glimpsed in the orb. Lightning crackled at its peak, and the air was thrumming with electricity.

"This is where the rift is," Kye whispered. "But be warned, the shadows here will test you."

Avery's heart pounded as they began their ascent. The climb was gruelling, the path littered with jagged rocks and treacherous ledges. As they neared the summit, the shadows coalesced into a towering figure – a monstrous being with shifting, amorphous features. It spoke in a voice that reverberated through her bones.

"Why do you seek to mend what is broken? The rift exists because of you."

Avery froze, the words cutting deep. Memories she had buried long ago surfaced – moments of regret, failure, and pain. The shadow loomed closer, feeding on her self-doubt.

"It's lying," Kye growled, positioning himself between Avery and the shadow. "You are more than your past. More than what you think." Kye stared into her eyes, and for a moment Avery got lost in them. *It can't be?* she thought to herself. Looking into Kye's eyes reminded her of someone. Someone she had lost. Someone she was not able to save when the soldiers came looking. Kaedyn.

Avery clenched her fists, her mind racing. She had spent so long running from her mistakes, but perhaps it was time to face them. She took a step forward, her voice steady. "I may have stumbled, but I am not defined by my failures. I didn't mean for him to die."

The shadow faltered, its form flickering. Emboldened, Avery pressed on. "I've seen the beauty in the Dreaming, the endless possibilities. I won't let fear destroy it."

With those words, the shadow let out a deafening roar before disintegrating into a cascade of dust. The rift in the fabric of dreams became visible, pulsing with chaotic energy. Avery could see the real world on the other side. She could see him. Her heart ached as she knew it was not possible. He was gone.

"Now, Avery," Kye urged. "You must seal it with your intent!"

Avery closed her eyes, focusing on the harmony she often experienced in her dreams. Imagining the face of someone she had once loved who she never thought she would see again. Who she had seen on the other side of the tear, always just out of reach. She imagined the rift mending, the chaos giving way to balance. When she opened her eyes, the rift was gone, and there was silence.

Avery awoke with a start, her heart still racing. Morning sunlight streamed through her window, casting golden patterns on her bed. She felt a profound sense of peace, as if a weight had been lifted.

A sharp knock on the door had her bolt upright, reaching for the fire poker that lay beside her on the dirty floor. It was always close by, in case the soldiers found her again. Peering through the window, Avery saw a familiar face. Kaedyn.

Racing to the door, she pulled Kaedyn in, his lips finding hers straight away as they crashed together in their embrace.

"I thought you were dead?" Avery cried, when they finally pulled apart, panting.

"When the soldiers came, I thought I was dead too. As we were running, you managed to open a dream rift, and I was pulled in. I watched as you kept running, not realising straight away that I was no longer following."

"I thought the soldiers got you. I've never been able to forgive myself."

"No, I was trapped in the Dreaming. I've been trying to find you ever since and last night, you mended the rift, and I was able to come home. To you."

Jenny England

Jenny England worked for many years as a freelance journalist. Now retired, living in Kiama, she is concentrating on mastering the art of the short story. In 2021 she won the Nadia Lyne Competition for Children's Writing and she has collected a few awards over the years. When not writing she can be found designing and knitting for charities

Endless Night

by Jenny England

Half awake

Not fully recovered from the comfort of sleep

And dreams of endless nights

With you beside me, once again

Awake.

Now conscious of the light that beckons

From the slits between the slats

Of the shutters on my bedroom wall

But you're not here

Now minutes feel like hours

Hours, an eternity of emptiness

'Til night returns again

Dozing

Not fully released from the pain of endless day ... but

Listening

For the sound of footsteps on the stairs

Not there. Again.

Watching

As darkness swallows up the slits between the slats

Of the shutters on my bedroom wall

Asleep

Now fully released

And dreaming of an endless night

With you beside me, once again

Melissa Shoard

Melissa Shoard is a book lover, singer, cake baker, music maker, theatre nerd, and never really fancied herself a writer but is a big believer in having a go at anything one might enjoy. She works in disability and lives in regional NSW with her funny husband, two gorgeous kids, two goofy dogs, countless fish and spiders, and as many reptiles as hubby can get away with.

Expectation

by Melissa Shoard

Whenever I heard anyone ask, "What are your goals in life? What's the dream?" I always kinda felt that maybe I was a bit ambitionless, because I didn't really have any. Nothing solid in my head anyway.

I never set a particular career or anything, and I've always been happy to go along with my job or family life. But it's interesting what you don't realise, and how badly you want something until it doesn't happen for you.

I guess I always just assumed I'd grow up, get married, and have a few kids. It's what everyone does, right? It's how all the stories end, and what I'd seen all around me.

My current self has a much better understanding of the beauty and brilliance of diversity and choice, but I digress.

Skip forward to me having the discussion with my husband about whether we did actually want children and when we would try to make that happen. And this is the journey I want to share.

I will preface this with the acknowledgment that I say all the following from a place of privilege, where I have had access to the resources and support I needed to achieve my dream, and that in the bigger picture, mine was not the longest or most arduous journey.

But, I'm a believer that all stories matter, and I do think this topic should be encouraged to be something we talk more about.

Infertility affects so many more people than we realise, (you only need to look at the worldwide explosion of social media following the airing of the Bluey episode *Onesies*, that addressed infertility, to see how many people have been touched by this), and we need love and support to feel seen, and to get through it.

I send all my love-and-support vibes out into the world to any and all going through it, at any level. I am in absolute awe of those monumentally strong people who battle for years on end.

This topic is hard.

It hurts.

I know several people in my various circles who have experienced difficulty (or inability) getting pregnant, miscarriages, very high risk pregnancies, and loss of children. I do think that as a society, we're getting a lot better at understanding and talking about these things, and our amazing medical minds are always discovering new ways to help. So much as I am wanting to share some difficult stuff here, I absolutely write with hope.

As I said, mine is not the hardest story, but here it is:

I have been blessed with two amazing little humans, and I am forever thankful for them. But it didn't just happen.

My first obstacle was a chronic illness, which meant a good 12-18 months of medical visits just to get stable enough for the doctor to approve us starting to try. This in itself was tedious enough (especially when one must travel for these appointments), each time hoping to be given the green light, but often not. So, I would go home feeling that I just have to put my life plans on hold for another few months until some guy says I can do what I want, with my body.

I remember how excited I was when I finally got the go-ahead. The thrill and the hopeful anticipation of a potential little line on the pee-stick.

Sure, I tried not to expect it to happen immediately, we all know, realistically, how unlikely that is. Except of course for those people I knew who had succeeded first try, or hadn't even been trying at all … surely I had a chance at that too?

A little over a year's worth of regular appointments for my health, always asking where things were up to … always having to say there was no news … trying to stay positive because for some unknown (even to me) reason I couldn't possibly let my doctor know how miserable we were about it … Emotions are weird.

Then began the visits with the fertility clinic. They were all the most amazing lovely people. I'm so grateful for the work they do. But nobody wants to have to go there. It's hard. And it's very, very expensive (I won't go into the extra stress and hardship that can cause for a lot of people).

For me it meant a lot of travel, early mornings, daily blood tests to track my cycle, drugs to boost all the hormones and processes, internal ultrasounds to see if the ovulation was happening as it should be, conversations about which days to have intercourse and then a waiting game to see if it had worked.

This was for both kids. At least I knew what to expect the second time, but we still had to try naturally for a while before we could go down this road.

Some cycles had to be abandoned as they just weren't going to work. Some looked good, leaving that little pill behind. And once you've done your very scheduled, very tired, and very unromantic date nights, you need two weeks to see if this time, maybe, it worked.

The waiting was one of the hardest parts. I don't have a regular 28-day cycle, more like 35-45 days, so between each failed attempt, I had a lot of waiting to be emotionally exhausted.

Waiting ... Hoping ... Wishing ...

Feeling like a failure.

Feeling like I was letting my husband down.

Feeling like I couldn't do the one biological job I was given as a woman.

One time after a failed cycle, I was waiting several weeks to be able to start all over again, and we were at a family gathering where someone had a gorgeous little newborn. I didn't know how much I wanted a baby in my arms until I found myself sitting a little way away, sobbing softly.

I couldn't go near that child or the parents in that moment. I did eventually, it's not their fault, and all was okay, but I'm at least glad I was able to identify in myself that I needed some processing time that day.

One day at the fertility clinic we unexpectedly ran into someone we knew – bit awkward at first. We were able to offer some understanding to them though, having been there before, and I think that helped. And we did have a good chat about the difficulty around how to talk to people about it, but also keep the level of privacy that you personally desire.

I'm still a bit amazed by the careless comments that come from people (sometimes friends, but usually people more on the fringe – workmates, a friend's mother, people in a group you attend), who seem to think the questions and comments are harmless:

"So when are you having kids?"

"Oh, you don't want to leave it too late!"

"When are you going to have another?"

"He'll need a playmate now."

And once you announce a pregnancy, "Congratulations! Was it planned?" ... I find this one particularly odd. When did *that* become a thing people feel they need to know?

There's a lot of societal history here, which I have no business trying to unpack. I just want to share my story and spread a bit of awareness.

I'm very fortunate that my story has a happy ending.

I got my kids, without too much waiting. I love them, and they're happy and healthy.

I still don't know what my goals or dreams are. Maybe I'm back to not having any. Or maybe they've changed to that overwhelming, joyous, exhausting, wonderful, stressful, and rewarding task of trying to raise good humans and make their dreams come true, whilst trying to stay true to yourself and your own expectations at the same time.

But that's a whole other story.

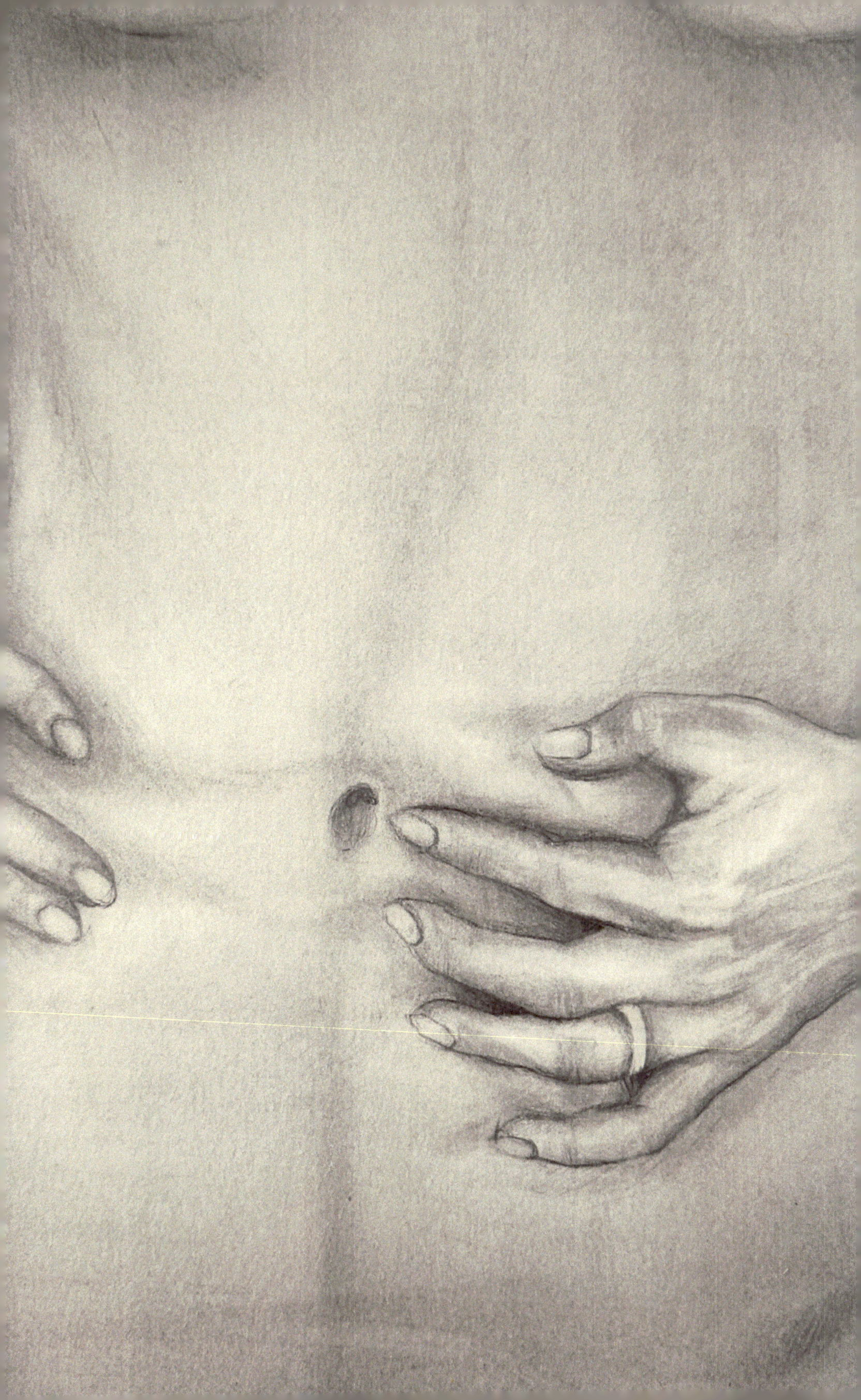

Margaret Onus

Margaret Onus takes everyday life experiences and includes them in her creative writing process. She has been published previously in *Senior Stories*, through NSW Government and FAW. Her interest areas in writing are memoir and disabilities, and seeks to write characters who overcome their barriers, both physical or emotional, drawing from her work experiences in the rehabilitation field.

Chasing a Dream

by Margaret Onus

Maggie and her elder sister, Grace, enjoyed an easy relationship, but both knew it was not the same with their younger sister, Helen. They dreamed of an improved relationship with her, even just a little.

Maggie was curious if meeting over lunch would give her a glimpse into the road blocks that continually seemed to mar the interactions. Her internal pent-up frustration bubbled out through her feet, urgently tapping against the floor as she considered problem solving approaches.

She would text:

> Would you like to have lunch together when I am next up North, week beginning 5th May?

A quick response back:

> sure

> Which day is better, Wednesday or Thursday?

> wednesday

The specific place would be left until she was in the area and could check some options.

With the lunch date set, Maggie was quietly surprised by how easy it had been. The exchange of texts seemed like an answer, a simple way at present to manage communication with Helen.

Their track record on phone calls had experienced multiple hiccups. At the last scheduled Zoom call, she hadn't logged in.

Her simple response to a follow-up text was:

forgot

A lapse again, she dismissed the thought. Maggie had already tagged Helen, in her own mind at least, as consistently Inconsistent – CIC.

Grace was, like her name, a flexible personality and an easy going sibling.

Helen, by contrast, seemed secretive and distant ever since she moved to Queensland. It had not been long after that move that she had become even more guarded, as she executed their parent's estate.

The irony was she had been quite persuasive to her parents to appoint her to the executive role, but her ambivalence was palpable initially, then followed angry and rude communications.

The evening before the luncheon Maggie's phone pinged with Helen's text. She asked:

what are the details for tomorrow?

Maggie sent a text with a map and pin drop for the club.

Next morning, after a cold dawn, the fog lifted and the sun warmed the day. With clear blue sky overhead, and the promise of a beautiful day, Maggie dressed in her black trousers and new red top.

Was the weather a sign of what the day would bring?

Google maps showed the direct route, and soon she was pulling in at the car park. She was just ready to enter the club when her phone pinged with a text:

As she signed in, Maggie asked, "Where would I find your Chinese restaurant?"

The doorman replied, "Five kms up the road at our sister venue."

"Consistent Inconsistent strikes again," she sighed as she googled the new directions and sent a quick text back:

Soon she was driving into the multi-level car park with the busy lunch rush. She followed another car through the maze of ramps and levels and together they found just two vacant spots in the back row.

She resolved not to say anything about the venue misread, while she paused for the other car to park before reversing into her space.

Maggie spotted Helen hovering a little way inside from the front sign in counter, not exactly close to the Chinese restaurant. She smiled, both at seeing her and registering surprise that she was wearing the same outfit, red long-sleeved top and black trousers.

There was a point of difference, that would not have been on any memo, bling accessories sparkling to outshine the sunlight on the nearby Gold Coast.

"Hi," Maggie said as she reached out to embrace Helen. "Did you get the family memo on dress code?"

Her response was muted. In fact, it almost seemed she was miffed by the family memo comment.

Instead, after an awkward little chuckle Helen said, "How are you? Did you have trouble finding a car park?"

"Well, I was in luck, I got the last spot, back row, against the pillars. So, do you know this club well? Where would you suggest we eat? Is the Chinese Restaurant good?" Maggie asked as they headed towards the lifts.

They walked through the food hall where the aroma of cooking pizza wafted by, creating a welcoming vibe.

"Do you fancy sharing a pizza?" asked Maggie as they found a table.

"That's fine," Helen said and picked up the menu to study it, while Maggie stood, checking if a glass of chardonnay was okay and sauntering off to get drinks.

Once the order was placed, curiously and carefully, Maggie enquired about Helen's welfare. Grace had mentioned that Helen felt there was no family link apart from sharing the same birth parents who were now long deceased.

Maggie wondered if Helen's difficult attitude had been triggered by management of issues in their parent's estate. Had the task developed into a complex long trail nightmare?

"How have you been since we last met up?" she asked. "Did you get to do that trip to Singapore?"

"No, I am still trying to line it up, as there are now extra travel options," Helen replied before turning the conversation back, asking, "How have you been lately?"

"Well as you know I have just come from the Book Fair Conference, which turned out to be rather fun as well as educational. I loved the speakers who showcased the breadth of memoir writing. You know, it seems everyone can have a story to tell," Maggie said. "You need to write a journey experience and explain your life lesson. For example, 'poverty to plenty, know your worth', 'chaotic childhood to corporate chief, lesson's from mates'. I think I would write 'small shack to money-pit mansion, home builder mistakes'. What would you say?" She paused and studied her sister's face.

"Dreary Days to Dream Days," Helen said after a few moments of reflection. "I am not interested in family, history, present or past, so I probably would leave the inside pages blank."

"No photo even of your beautiful fur baby, Romulus?" Maggie asked, picking a safe topic. Then, "Do you want this last pizza piece?" she offered, pushing the platter towards Helen. "What does interest you then?"

Helen munched on the melted cheese mix. "Moving to Queensland was my life transition point. I dreamt of a different life and I don't feel I need to be accountable to any of the family for the past," she replied. "Living here, I enjoy my theatre group, we just saw 'Sister Act' recently. It was a wonderful show, great story.

Absolutely amazing!" She waved her hands theatrically. "Have you seen it?"

"No, but I hope to later this year," said Maggie.

The conversation moved along around books and films then slid back to Maggie's holiday adventures much like a cherry tomato in salad dressing. Maggie wondered if the Sister Act reference could be a metaphor about her move to Queensland, her own version of escape, a dream for distance or secrecy.

She finished her meal, only partially comforted by the food and company. Maggie left the table to order two pots of tea from the café, and an apple slice to share.

Returning, she said, "Okay, maybe I should count myself fortunate that you came for lunch, thanks for joining me, I don't really understand your desire for disconnect of family."

"It's nice to see you," Helen offered gently.

Maggie could suddenly see the pebbles of conversation given were little gifts to keep the pathway open but there was a drawbridge nearby ready to close if needed.

Helen broke the tension by suggesting they head to the foyer and take a photograph at the state boundary line.

Maggie wondered again if this was a warning message, this state boundary is her zone – Don't Cross – or another form of veto over connection.

That done, they bid their farewells with a promise of another catchup ... but no specifics.

Maggie felt in her spirit that the desire for bonding was a fading shimmering shadow, much like a whisp of smoke escaping out the open window.

Only the higher order universal all-knowing dream angel could know what had really occurred in the affairs of the estate – and in her sister's life – over the last thirty or more years.

She certainly was not going to give any clues of adventure or otherwise, trauma or hardships and besides no one was asking. It is the past, and will continue to remain there.

She returned to her car and edged out of the car park.

Lunch had been a sandwich experience, a meeting between curiosity and a nightmare.

She recalled the adage, "be careful what you wish for," as she blinked hard twice pushing down her sad tears, and released her heart's desire.

Driving home, she let her lost dream escape through the window.

She called Grace from the car, to debrief.

"Our dream would be Helen's worst nightmare," she said. "I'm letting it go, it's been a wake-up meeting, waking up is a gift, a different view."

Anonymous

Anonymous has been voted Most Likely To:
be off writing something sassy
using a pseudonym .

Reality Bites

by Anonymous

Not in my right mind?
Insanity! Reality shatters online,
cracked reality like a spider-webbed smart screen
while AI becomes more real
than "IRL". We all dream of being better
than our forefathers. Are we better?
Better is as better does, so I fear not,
within this reality.

Posh! Who says I live in a lessened "true world"
from choosing to ignore the media,
claims of waking dreams crumbling
and the emergence of nightmares
made real:
Wars fought without and within,
gaols filled,
courts chock-full of children,
crimes against a humanity who forgot
how to dream,
simply,
of happiness.

Hope, a guiding light, winks at me
as if from across an ocean
– like Gatsby, dreaming of his Lady Love –
only life is not an endless party.
No glitter shines here.
No. I taste bitter and see sour
faced paranoia all around.

They look but do not see,
and I am irrelevant to this reality?
Posh!
Let me crawl back into my cave then,
carve out dreams on cold stone walls,
return to Mother Earth and curl into her warm womb.

Let me breathe in the damp soil,
and feel the fire in my boiling blood
as it slowly,
slowly,
simmers down.

Phoebe Ginnivan

Phoebe has an innate connection to the natural world and enjoys creative outlets. Phoebe can often be found taking nature walks, spending oodles of quality/busy time with her toddler and relishing in a Sunday morning Yoga class. Her work brings light to the quiet corners of life, like snowflakes and colours that aren't always seen.

Scam

by Phoebe Ginnivan

I must be dreaming,

Because they're scheming.

To take the land

& give it to man.

Not to the ones who know it best,

But to the ones,

With heartless chests.

R.M. Mooreland

R.M. Mooreland is a writer who finds inspiration in the melodies of life and the landscapes that surround her. When not writing, she can be found wandering in forests, listening to her latest musical discovery, or losing herself in the worlds of the books she loves.

Living the Dream

by R.M. Mooreland

Science tells us that when we dream, our brains are doing one of several things, including:

1. Consolidating memories: Sorting and storing important events, thoughts and feelings.

2. Emotional processing: Learning from emotional experiences, rehearsing emotional responses, and working through significant emotional experiences.

3. Unconscious expression: Dreams may represent our deepest thoughts, desires, wants, needs and motivations.

4. Problem solving: Processing how we face, or how we plan to face, certain problems or situations.

To 99.99999993% of people on Earth, these things are true.

But what Science doesn't tell us is what the other 0.00000003% of people know: That dreams can be portals to other worlds.

It's a privileged and VERY well-kept secret known to only 547 people out of the 8.2 billion living on Planet Earth. Well, *this* version of Planet Earth. And you're about to get a first-hand account of what happens when a dream world and a reality world cross over.

Let me start from the beginning.

I, Sibel Greene, am one of the 0.00000003%. When I sleep, my dreams transport me to other worlds, where I'm responsible for helping the Sprites, the protectors of the natural world and the magic that defines and sustains their realms. They are the connection between the dream worlds and the reality worlds.

So why me? What makes me one of only 547 people with the ability to visit the dream worlds?

The lore says that Sprites can choose to bestow their magic on worthy individuals, giving them the ability to travel to the dream worlds. This gift is not bestowed lightly. It must be earned.

In the Real World, Sprites are largely considered mythical creatures of legend and lore. Made up fairy-like creatures designed to teach children lessons about protecting our delicate ecosystems. Well, guess what, they're not myth – they're real. You just don't know until you've earned the privilege of seeing them. My ability was passed down from my ancestors, just like all of us with the gift.

When I was growing up, my dad would tell me stories about how his ancestor, Aine, transformed the lives of her family forever, when she saved an ancient Irish Oak from being felled for lumber. The tree had stood for 1000 years, witnessing the passing of time with steadfast strength and grace. It's twisted roots stretched far, forming intricate connections with the forest around it.

The tree had become the heart and soul of the forest, responsible for keeping the delicate balance that encouraged life to flourish within. In turn, the forest gifted the tree with nourishment so that it could grow tall and healthy.

Aine had loved this tree from the time she was a girl. She would sit under its vast canopy and speak with it, sometimes even sing to it. She would climb its strong branches and feel its bark beneath her soft hands, almost able to feel a heartbeat. She couldn't explain the connection she felt when she was with the tree.

The Oak Tree was safe.

The Oak Tree was home.

The Sprites watched as the girl grew from a child to a beautiful young woman, visiting the Oak Tree every day. They watched her fall in love and get married under the protective embrace of its branches. They bore witness to the birth of her three children, supported by its strong roots. And they grieved with her the day her eldest son was killed by a warrior from an invading clan, her hot tears soaking into the soil, the tree's immovable trunk supporting her body, the wind in the leaves carrying her pain away as she wailed. She buried him there, his body becoming part of the tree, forever preserving his soul.

The Sprites watched as the clan war raged on.

Two years went by.

Three.

Four.

The forest around them began to dwindle as the people cut more and more trees down for barricades and weaponry, and to replace burned houses. The Oak Tree's connections to the forest were severed as its roots were forced to release the entanglement holding fast to the now naked stumps surrounding it. It began to wilt and die, and the growing desperation of the clan's people saw them looking to fell the great Oak Tree.

The Sprites were distraught. Desperate.

Knowing that cutting down the wise tree, the soul of the forest would be extinguished forever and the Sprites would die along with it. The forest would become a baren plain.

Aine stood in front of the great tree, refusing to move aside. She cried for her son, her first born, and begged the clan not to destroy his soul. Her husband and her remaining son and daughter joined her in her plea, appealing to the clan to leave their son, their brother, their tree, unharmed. They told the clan that they would devote their lives to resisting the invading clans, they would find ways to protect the village without destroying the Oak Tree. The clan took pity, and took them at their word.

The Sprites watched. They watched Aine and her family work tirelessly to find other sources of lumber and food to support the village. They watched as the family planted seedlings around the Oak Tree with loving hands to replace what was taken. The Sprites imbued the seedlings with magic to help them grow. And when Aine died, her body buried with her son at the base of the great tree, daisies grew that miraculously never died.

The clan wars eventually ended, the village intact, but the forest broken. The Sprites watched Aine's son and daughter grow and find love of their own, each marrying and starting families themselves. The Sprites decided that the sacrifice of Aine and her children was worthy of their gift, but only if they birthed their children at the base of the tree, as Aine had done all those years ago. Cora, Aine's daughter, birthed two girls under the watchful gaze of the Sprites and the protection of the Oak Tree.

As each baby was born, the Sprites each took turns to touch the baby and gift it with a small amount of Sprite magic. They did the same for Aine's son, Barclay's children when he brought his wife to the tree to birth their children, two boys and a girl. This gift allowed the children to see the Sprites, and they began having vivid dreams of wonderful places.

The Sprites would lead them through beautiful forests, swim in sparkling waters with them, run deer trails and roll down grassy hills.

One day, when the children were old enough, the Sprites began to take them to other places. Places that weren't beautiful. Places that were hurt, places that were filled with pain and sadness. The Sprites needed their help. They were tasked with helping to restore peace to these worlds, and to help heal and regenerate the forests, woodlands, plains, oceans, rivers, lakes.

With each successful dream, the Oak Tree grew strong and healthy once more, reconnecting the forest network and restoring balance to nature. With this gift came responsibilities that would be passed down from generation to generation, but only those with pure hearts would live the gift, live the dreams.

Aine was my great, great, great, great, great, great ... Well, you get it ... she's OLD! And I must be pure of heart, because I have had the gift since I can remember. Her legacy lives on – in me.

So why do you need to know all of this? It helps for you to have some context, because I have a slight problem. Actually, it's more of a Sprite problem.

You see, I've accidentally brought back a Nymph from a dream world ... and I'm in big trouble.

Here I am, laying flat on my face with a steaming pile of dog poo inches from my nose, my knee smarting with pain from the rock it just landed on, my shoelaces tied firmly together, watching the Nymph about to enact a plan to make a woman on a bike ride straight into a lake, before undoubtedly moving on to her next victim. Nymphs. Tricksters, every single one of them!

The problem is, if I don't get the Nymph back to her own dream by the next time I need to sleep, the portal to her dream world will be open to my reality. Our reality. If reality mixes with dreams, if those two worlds collide, people living in reality will become trapped in an eternal nightmare that they can never awaken from, and the dream world ceases to exist all together.

So you see, my shoelaces, the dog poo and my busted up knee, are quite the least of my problems ... OUR problems. Those dreams you've been having, where you always find that same horse to gallop along that beach with? That's real. It's not just your heart's biggest wish.

You're in a dream world.

You have the gift.

And I need your help.

B.D. Roy

B.D. Roy writes stories that truly resonate with today's youth. A teacher taught him the value of "writing about what you know." This approach inspired him to capture the real struggles and dreams of everyday youngsters. Living by the sea on the NSW Central Coast, his creative spirit is as vast as the ocean he loves.

Dreams of the Ancestors

by B.D. Roy

Jila Guda, an isolated town, lies nestled between ancient gums and deep-water holes, an oasis in the heart of the Australian desert. Where the earth holds stories like echoes of ancestors resonating within the heartbeats of the land.

The town's stillness murmurs with the whispers of those who walked here long before, their steps etched in the dust. The pull of this place was inevitable for Kalina after the passing of her grandmother, Yindi. Her spirit now wandered the same tracks as the ancestors who had gone before.

Kalina, twenty-three, was a woman shaped by the world's harshness, yet something shifted upon her return to this vast, dry land, to this place of her mob, the place of her origin. It was a shift she couldn't name, a stirring deep within her, as though the land itself had reached out to touch her spirit, awakening something old and restless.

The nights following her return were filled with dreams unlike any she had known before. These were not mere dreams; they were journeys, voyages through time, to a place where memory and spirit entwined.

Through eyes not her own, Kalina saw a life that pulsed with emotions, foreign yet familiar, a life not hers, yet tied to her blood.

The dreams were fragments at first, disjointed glimpses into a world she could barely comprehend. But as the days stretched into weeks, the visions fused, their clarity sharpening like the edge of a blade, drawing her deeper into a past that seemed to rise from the earth beneath her feet.

Each deep breath Kalina took filled her lungs with the weight of what had come before. Her days passed in a kind of trance, her mind circling the dreams like an animal on the hunt, searching for meaning in the images that haunted her.

While sorting through her grandmother's belongings, Kalina's fingers brushed against an old scrapbook, its cover cracked and brittle, the pages yellowed with age. The book had belonged to her great-grandmother, Kirra, who she had heard was a woman revered for being the trusted keeper of her mob's stories, a strong woman, not someone to mess with. Kalina's breath caught as she opened the book, the scent of time and memory rising from its pages.

Inside, the scrapbook was a tapestry of her great-grandmother's journeys, woven together with faded pages, photographs, clippings, and stories penned in a hand that trembled with age yet remained steady in its purpose. As Kalina turned the pages, a sense of familiarity washed over her. The faces, the places, everything aligned with the dreams that had invaded her sleep.

With the turning of each page, Kalina felt herself sinking deeper into the past, the connection growing stronger with every word, every image. It was as though she was living Kirra's, life, feeling her joys, her sorrows, her loves, and her losses.

The line between dreaming and waking blurred, where Kalina found herself adrift in a world where time had no meaning, where the past reached out to claim her.

Each night the dreams grew more intense, weaving themselves into the very fabric of Kalina's mind. Each dream brought Kirra's life into sharper focus, the joyous echoes of her childhood laughter, the heavy mantle of leadership she bore, and a forbidden love that transcended the harsh boundaries of her time.

Kirra had fallen in love with Michael, a young man from a white farming family, a love that blazed fiercely despite the era's cruel realities. Their union was blessed with a daughter, Yindi, who filled their lives with pride, but the community was unforgiving.

When the authorities came to take their daughter away, Michael fought with all his strength to hold her tight. The struggle ended in tragedy, Michael was taken in front of Kirra, his life extinguished in an instant. On that fateful day, Kirra lost her devoted husband and their daughter, leaving her heart shattered.

Kalina's days were consumed by her search for answers, for the secrets hidden in Kirra's book and the depths of her dreams. But with each step she took toward the unknown, a darkness began to creep into her dreams. She felt Kirra's most painful moments, relived her betrayals, her losses, her grief that cut so deep it left wounds that never healed. The nightmares left Kalina shaken, questioning whether she should continue reading.

Yet something deep within her refused to let go.

Kirra had written about a hidden cave, a place the elders spoke of in whispers, a sacred ground where the ancestors painted their stories on the cave walls to be passed on to other generations.

With her backpack slung over her shoulder, Kalina followed Kirra's directions to the ancestral cave.

The entrance was narrow, almost invisible beneath the tangled bush, but Kalina found it as if guided by an unseen hand. The air inside was cool, the scent of earth and time thick in her nostrils. Her torch flickered as she stepped deeper into the interior, the beam of light revealing ancient drawings, stories painted on stone by hands long gone.

Kirra's map led her to a rock painting of a boomerang. As she reached it, Kalina's heart pounded. Placing the torch on a nearby ledge, she knelt beneath the rock painting and began to dig, the earth yielding beneath her bare hands.

Then, her fingers brushed against something solid, a rectangular box, its surface worn by time but preserved by the dry desert sand. The box was locked, but Kalina knew she had uncovered something that held the secrets of Kirra's past. She gathered the box under her arm and quickly exited the cave.

That night, the dream returned, more vivid than ever. Kalina was no longer herself; she was Kirra, standing inside the mission church, a place heavy with sorrow and pain. In the dream, Kirra was desperate, her hands trembling as she hid something precious beneath the altar floorboards. Kalina watched through Kirra's eyes, feeling the urgency, the fear, and the hope that had driven her to this act. The vision was so clear, so real, that when Kalina woke, she knew she had to go to the mission church to understand its purpose.

At first light, Kalina quickly dressed and made her way to the mission church on the edge of town, its once proud structure now in disrepair. Despite this, the altar was untouched, covered in desert dust, and forgotten by time. With a sense of reverence, she knelt behind the altar where she found and removed a loose floorboard. Beneath it lay a rusty, tarnished key, just as the dream had shown her.

Her heart raced as she hurried home, the key fitting perfectly into the box's lock. With a soft click, the lid opened, revealing a letter and an intricately carved wooden boomerang, its surface adorned with symbolic stories of her ancestors, each carving a thread in the tapestry of the past.

Kalina unfolded the letter, fragile with age. It was addressed to the one who would find it, a message from Kirra to her daughter or one of her descendants. The letter spoke not of conflict or material needs, but of a legacy of love, resilience, and forgiveness.

Kirra had written of her hopes for the future, urging those who came after her to cherish their roots, take pride in their heritage, learn from the past but not be bound by it.

Kirra explained that the dreams were a message of love, leading Kalina to this moment of understanding, showing her that the true treasure was not what the box contained, but the strength and spirit of her ancestors carried through the ages.

A deep sense of closure filled Kalina as she finished reading the letter.

The dreams stopped, but their absence did not leave her empty. Instead, she felt their presence more strongly than ever, as though her ancestors were with her still, guiding her steps.

The people of Jila Guda, moved by Kirra's story, voted to honour this legacy. They envisioned a great boomerang, not just as a replica of the one found, but as a lasting symbol for mankind. The local youth group, enthused by the idea, took on this task. Youngsters working as one, with hands steady and hearts full pride. Etching the ancient patterns with care, as if tracing the very lines of past stories and future dreams.

When they raised it in the heart of the town where it stood not merely as a proud monument, but as the breath of their ancestors, whispering of forgiveness, of unity – a beacon for all who sought understanding and reconciliation.

As the sun was setting over the horizon Kalina made her way up the hill and sat overlooking the town. The day was ending, she watched as the last rays of the sun stretch out across the red earth and slowly fade away, but within her, a new chapter was beginning. She knew that the dreams of her ancestors would live on, not just in the town's past, but in its future.

Kalina smiled, feeling at one with the land, her ancestors, her family, and the dreams that had led her to this moment.

The boomerang, a symbol of Jila Guda's shared history, still stands proud and tall as a testament to ancient stories passed down through the ages, a reminder of the town's journey of understanding, forgiveness, healing, and hope for their future.

Keep
Dreamin'

Acknowledgements

Wattle Tree Press began with a five-year-old girl, an encouraging kindergarten teacher, a lead pencil, and a dream that one day she might grow up to be an author. Over the years, that childhood wish came true, but it didn't stop there, with the young author's goals evolving into a bigger publishing dream that is still evolving today.

I am proud to say that our journey as authors and publishers has only just begun here at Wattle Tree Press, but we cannot wait to see how it continues to grow into the future.

2025 brought with it a lot of learning curves and some amazing people to our publishing family.

We'd like to acknowledge them here.

Firstly, the development of this anthology would not have been possible without the **amazing authors** you will discover within the pages of this book.

We are so proud to represent these creative writers and their work in our anthology. These authors used their words to draw us in and make us *feel.* Some are seasoned writers. Others are not. But each entrant bravely entered our competition, trusted us with their words, and allowed us to share their work. Without them, this anthology would not be possible. It has been a labour of love, and these authors have patiently awaited publication.

Thank you (in order of appearance) to: Natalie Bock, Glenda Morgan, Jess Senff, Sandra Taylor, Paris Rosemont, C.J. Garth, The Sisterhood of the Travelling Story, Laura Honeysett, Jessica Giblin Jobson, Wen Gibson, Brendan Gulson, Carlyn Smith, Bronwyn Boehm, Dorothy Swoope, Glofernwolfe, Jorvn Jones, Tara Jean, Jenny England, Melissa Shoard, Margaret Onus, Anonymous, Phoebe Ginnivan, R.M. Moreland, and B.D. Roy.

Secondly, many thanks go to the **talented artists and illustrators** whose work is also featured in this anthology.

These creatives answered the call to create an original piece of art to compliment an entry and wow did they deliver! In a range of mediums, they shared their talent with paper and pencil, watercolour, or with digital drawing software, and we have been blown away. Opening snail mail and email to find your art has made this journey even more fun! We are grateful that you took up your implement of choice and created something beautiful to breathe life into this anthology.

Thank you to The Art Witch, Lisa A. Kennedy, Glofernwolfe, and Pip Huckle.

We are so proud to showcase these artists in this anthology. Their art moved us with colour and line, bringing the 'dreaming' to life. Without them, this anthology would not be as beautiful.

Many thanks also go to the people behind the scenes – to Tara for editing, Louise for proofreading, the team behind the cover design, and the partners and children who gave us the time and peace to work, the baristas who hooked up the IV and trickle-fed us coffee when we needed it (joking! though, what a dream *that* is!) ...

Lastly, I wish to thank *you*, dear reader, for holding this anthology in your hands right now. We hope these words and artwork inspire you and your continued dreaming.

About the Artists

Artwork: Expectation

Pip is a passionate illustrator with a diverse style that shifts from playful and colourful to clean and intricate, with her work reflecting her love for experimenting with different techniques.

Over the years, she's been selected to showcase in competitions such as Young in Art, gaining valuable experience and recognition. She is eager to take her skillset to the next level. Pip is particularly passionate about creating art for authors, committed to creating visually captivating art that compliments compelling stories.

You can find Pip on Instagram @pip.huckle

Artwork: Dawn of Flight

The Art Witch is a mysterious young woman who left an artwork of a phoenix on a scroll after a coin was thrown into a well ...

She resides amongst the rural green lands of the Central Coast, drawing and doodling and perfecting her craft, surrounded by horses and dogs with too much personality.

LISA A. KENNEDEY

Artwork: Mother Koala

Lisa A. Kennedy is an artist, veterinarian and children's book illustrator who describes her art as an ever-present undercurrent in her life. Her business 'Art By Lisa' primarily resulting in the creation of realistic depictions of native Australian birds and wildlife.

After becoming a mother to two little girls, she felt inspired to redirect her artistic talents to the world of children's book illustrating.

Lisa works in pen, ink and watercolour to create her delightfully whimsical and charming original illustrations.

See more of Lisa's artwork at https://artbylisa.com.au/

GLOFERNWOLFE

Artwork: Terror Kitchen

Glofernwolfe is a writer and a self-taught artist whose work blends futuristic dystopia with grounded realism. Growing up in India, he travelled widely—from the chaotic pulse of industrial metropolises like Mumbai to the majestic stillness of the snowy Himalayas. These contrasting landscapes reflect strongly in the worlds he builds in his writing and art.

Since moving to Australia in 2018, Glofernwolfe has published works on Tapas and Globalcomix, earning a loyal readership. His notable projects include *The Adventures of Zovhara Ashfrost*, a sci-fi web novel, and an upcoming cyberpunk graphic novel, *A Symphony of Rust and Snow*.

Explore Glofernwolfe's work via his link tree at: https://linktr.ee/glofernwolfe

More About the Authors

WEN GIBSON

Wen Gibson, author of the powerful and empowering memoir, *Stammering Against Truth*, has given us a heartfelt story of what it's like to dream. She followed her dreams, travelling the world on a bicycle, settling in Scotland, then returning to the Central Coast where she is passionate about her work as a counsellor. At the core of her life is kindness. Her short story, *Dalek Learning*, was published in *The Pearl Prize, a Midsumma Pride* 2025 competition, and *Speaking through Dysfluency*, has been included in the *Seniors' Stories Volume 10*.

To find out more about Wen, visit her website at https://wengibson.com

DOROTHY SWOOPE

Dorothy Swoope is a widely published award-winning writer. Her publications include *The Touch of a Word, Moments of Distraction* and her childhood memoir *Wait 'til Your Father Gets Home!* She resides on the South Coast of New South Wales.

JENNY ENGLAND

Jenny England worked for many years as a freelance journalist. Now retired, living in Kiama, she is concentrating on mastering the art of the short story.

In 2021 she won the Nadia Lyne Competition for Children's Writing and has had most of her children's stories published in *The School Magazine*. Her adult's stories are now published in her local paper, magazines and anthologies, and she has collected a few awards over the years.

When not writing she can be found designing and knitting for charities.

PARIS ROSEMONT

Paris Rosemont is an Asian-Australian poet with a niche in theatrical performance poetry. Her debut poetry collection *Banana Girl* (WestWords, 2023) was shortlisted by the Association for the Study of Australian Literature for the 2024 Mary Gilmore Award. *Banana Girl* was also shortlisted for Poetry Book Awards 2024 in Australia, Greece and the UK, and awarded 'Distinguished Favorite' in the NYC Independent Press Award 2025 (USA). Paris's second poetry collection, *Barefoot Poetess*, was released in March 2025.

She can be found on Instagram @msparisrose

JESSICA SENFF

Jessica Senff writes MG and YA fantasy novels based in magical worlds and featuring strong young characters facing a variety of unique problems ... often involving evil sorcery! She loves when these individuals prevail, reminding the reader that solutions can often be found in life – with a little perseverance and good humour.

Jessica spends her days teaching science and maths in the Southern Tablelands of New South Wales, Australia. She lives with her husband, three children, four rescued shorthair felines, and a beleaguered Poodle x Border Collie.

You can find Jess on Facebook (Jess Senff Stories) and Instagram as @jesssenffstories

Connect with her via her website: https://www.jesssenffstories.com

THE SISTERHOOD OF THE TRAVELLING STORY

The Sisterhood of the Travelling Story is comprised of five long-term best friends who have been separated by the demands of adulthood, motherhood, and life beyond high school. The Sisterhood became a long-distance book club, then a collaborative writing group during the Covid lockdown era. Each sister would add a few hundred words before sending the story on to the next sister in the chain, to stay connected, creative, and to escape into magical worlds of their own creation. Now, they cherish their childhood connections while writing their own life stories.

Scattered across Australia, the Sisterhood continues to work through each real-life and fictional plot twist that's thrown their way.

BRONWYN BOEHM

Now living on NSW's beautiful north coast, Bronwyn Boehm has enjoyed several analytical careers in city and regional Australia, while writing throughout. Taking up freelance journalism in her recent retirement, she has published human interest pieces in regional newspapers, magazines and websites. But harping back to her first publishing success at age 8 years (a Spike Milligan-inspired limerick, SMH Sunday edition), Bronwyn is resurrecting her creative soul through fiction. Her true passion lies in writing short stories, with a competition first prize and several further anthology publications and commendations. Her quest is to immortalise the Australian psyche at its most basic and beautiful through quirky yet poignant tales.

LAURA HONEYSETT

Laura Honeysett immersed herself in stories growing up and always dreamed of becoming a storyteller which she explored through music, drama and short stories that she created for her nephews. Now as a loving mother of two active boys and passionate speech pathologist, Laura uses story in her everyday life, from teaching communication and literacy skills to compassionately supporting tricky behaviours and childhood development through story teaching.

You can find more of Laura's work at her website https://learningalongsideyou.com/

or follow her on Instagram @learning.alongside.you

B.D. ROY

B.D. Roy writes stories that truly resonate with today's youth. A teacher taught him the value of "writing about what you know." This approach inspired him to capture the real struggles and dreams of everyday youngsters. Living by the sea on the NSW Central Coast, his creative spirit is as vast as the ocean he loves. His writing, ranges from short stories to novels, like his easy-to-read YA Surfing novel *Impact Zone* speaks volumes about his dedication to authentic young adult storytelling.

CARLYN SMITH

Carlyn Smith is a young emerging author with a passion for storytelling and mental advocacy. Carlyn contributed to an anthology, focusing on Indigenous Dreamtime stories, blending in traditional narratives with modern concerns. Mother Koala is centered around the threatened wildlife caused by dry bushfires in Australia. Through vivid storytelling, Carlyn seeks to raise awareness about the environmental challenges affecting Australian wildlife, and to bring the audience a sense of empathy when it comes to our fury, marsupial friends. Carlyn thanks Wattle Tree Press for valuing the importance of this story, and bringing it to life.

You can find her on Instagram @ccaarlynnn

SANDRA TAYLOR

Sandra Taylor, writing of earth, heart and spirit, has had work published in magazines, created chapbooks and zines, spoken word performed at festivals and community events. Sandra has a BA in Professional Writing and works within the community on art, theatre, and poetry projects. Living in a forest in a mud brick castle immersed in birdsong she plays, creatively exploring the sacred and the mundane.

Sandra began blogging in 2012 and occasionally still posts. More recently she has moved to substack. Find Sandra Taylor @eartheartwise or thefaeriembassy.com

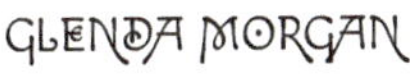

GLENDA MORGAN

Glenda Morgan is a poet and artist who resides on Yuin Country in Bermagui NSW. Her Chinese/Indigenous/Irish heritage influences her writing, giving refreshing experiences of connections to self and Earth. As an emerging poet, Glenda is an advocate for the previously unnoticed and neglected. She has had poems and artworks published in *Chasing the Lines: An Anthology* (2022) and is the creator of *ReGensis multi-media Installation* for poem/visual art (2023) with nationally and internationally exhibiting art for 30 years. Glenda is a Qigong/Buddhist practitioner of 27 years who organises and performs in community events, festivals and art galleries, and loves her dog.

TARA JEAN

Tara Jean is an emerging author with a talent for weaving heartfelt stories of love, second chances, spice and a little bit of feel-good and nice. Based in Brisbane, she draws inspiration from her passion for teaching and psychology, crafting characters and plots that resonate with readers on a deeply human level. A proud Wiradjuri woman, she is connected to her Aboriginal heritage and celebrates her culture through storytelling. She loves stargazing and researching anything related to First Nations science. When she's not working on her own novels or editing the amazing stories of other wonderful authors, Tara can be found at home cherishing time with her family and her beloved old doggy, finding joy in the simple moments that inspire her work.

BRENDAN GULSON

After dabbling with short stories and poetry in his younger years, Brendan Gulson really found his creative feet upon moving to the country in 2014. Inspired by a series of bizarre experiences that occurred in his valley, he wrote a short story that was included in an anthology of stories published by Wyong Shire Council. In 2023, he branched off into including cartoons and gothic imagery with his writings. He is gradually creating an outdoor gallery at his property, *Nevertime*, in the hinterland of the Central Coast of NSW. Brendan's writing and artwork is inspired by a deep-seated connection with the landscape and an ongoing interest in history and mysticism. He is currently wondering where all the Bohemians have gone.

NATALIE BOCK

Natalie Bock is a word addict who composes poetry and prose. A scribbler since she learned to write, she paused to raise her sons before returning to the writing scene in 2022. Since then, to her continuing astonishment, her words have found their way into five anthologies and a collection of short stories and won a poetry award. *Must Be Dreamin'* will be the seventh publication her writing has been included in. Natalie hopes never to wake from this delightful dream come true.

Follow her journey on Facebook or Instagram at nataliebock.wordaddict

R.M. MOORELAND

R.M. Mooreland is a writer who finds inspiration in the melodies of life and the landscapes that surround her. Whether exploring the sounds of a favourite song or the quiet rustle of leaves in the wind, Mooreland's writing is deeply intertwined with her love for both the natural world and the immersive, transformative power of fiction. When not writing, she can be found wandering in forests, listening to her latest musical discovery, or losing herself in the worlds of the books she loves.

R.M. Mooreland's stories invite readers to escape into vibrant realms, where music and nature meet the imagination in a harmonious dance.

 JORVN JONES

Jorvn Jones is primarily a writer, but, as a subset of Jorvn's writing practice, explores performance, theatre and film making, soundtracking and dance, and new media, incorporating sculptural installations and collages. Jorvn has extensive history as photographer and model. Jorvn's primary writing practice lays in poetry, but has encompassed essay and scriptwriting, blogging (social commentary/critique), and extending memoirs within online social context, in response to common themes in Jorvn's work. Jorvn has published in *Junky Scum, The MadHouse* collaborative artists' books, *cicatrix, Kooky Book Project, The Waiting Room anthology, Unsweetened Literary Journal, Sapphic Voyage* poetry journal, *Sapphocestors* anthology, in *Telescope Time... anthology*, and an obscure chapbook called *Vampire Tapeworms/Russian Tearooms,* which, if you can find a copy, you win a prize. Jorvn's work is archived at: https://www.youtube.com/@jorvnjones https://jorvnjonesfirstexpansion.tumblr.com https://soundcloud.com/jorvn_jones

 C.J. GARTH

C.J. Garth has always been captivated by the thrill of adventure and the magic of flight. With a passion for storytelling, C.J. enjoys weaving tales that spark curiosity and wonder. When not writing, C.J. loves spending time outdoors and is currently locked in a battle of wits with the birds stealing her strawberries. Whether exploring the skies in stories or immersing herself in the worlds of others, C.J. finds joy in the power of storytelling to inspire new experiences.

MELISSA SHOARD

Melissa Shoard is a book lover, singer, cake baker, music maker, theatre nerd, and never really fancied herself a writer but is a big believer in having a go at anything one might enjoy. She loves performing and singing with her choirs and loves a good chat. She works in disability and lives in regional NSW with her funny husband, two gorgeous kids, two goofy dogs, countless fish and spiders, and as many reptiles as hubby can get away with.

JESSICA GIBLIN JOBSON

Living on the sunny Central Coast, Jessica Giblin Jobson has always had a passion for writing, with many hours spent reading and creating her own stories. Her daughter, Amelia, has become the inspiration for her writing, creating a whole new realm of imagination to share with her. When she's not writing, Jessica enjoys time at the beach with her family, watercolour painting, and music.

ANONYMOUS

Anonymous has been voted *Most Likely To: Be Off Writing Something Sassy Using a Pseudonym.* They are also the recipient of the *Least Likely To: Use a Creative Nom de Plume Award.*

MARGARET ONUS

Margaret Onus takes everyday life experiences and includes them in her creative writing process. She has recently started retirement, enjoying additional free time for indulging her hobby. She has been published previously in *Senior Stories*, through NSW Government and FAW. Her interest areas in writing are memoir and disabilities, and seeks to write characters who overcome their barriers, both physical or emotional, drawing from her work experiences in the rehabilitation field.

PHOEBE GINNIVAN

Phoebe has an innate connection to the natural world and enjoys creative outlets. She can often be found taking nature walks, spending oodles of quality/busy time with her toddler and relishing in a Sunday morning Yoga class. Phoebe's work brings light to the quiet corners of life, like snowflakes and colours that aren't always seen, and she hopes to spark your curiosity with her writing style!

Phoebe first established her writing roots by studying a Bachelor in Communication, Majoring in Writing and Cultural Studies, at UTS. Her poetry was published in Vertigo, the University Magazine, and she has held multiple poetry exhibitions. Phoebe is currently juggling working as a casual teacher, whilst enjoying her Motherhood journey. Having written for US jewellery brand Bahgsu Jewels and self-publishing two poetry books, she is very passionate about the written word but can also be found at the odd poetry slam, giving a voice to the spoken word.

Connect with Phoebe on Instagram @foalandco, where she documents the parts of her life that ignite joy and explores the creative projects she loves to dabble in, uncovering the treasures found by being present to the wonders of the world around us.

GLOFERNWOLFE

Glofernwolfe is a writer and a self-taught artist whose work blends futuristic dystopia with grounded realism. Growing up in India, he travelled widely – from the chaotic pulse of industrial metropolises like Mumbai to the majestic stillness of the snowy Himalayas. These contrasting landscapes reflect strongly in the worlds he builds in his writing and art.

Since moving to Australia in 2018, Glofernwolfe has published works on Tapas and Globalcomix, earning a loyal readership. His notable projects include *The Adventures of Zovhara Ashfrost*, a sci-fi web novel, and an upcoming cyberpunk graphic novel, *A Symphony of Rust and Snow*.

Explore Glofernwolfe's work via his link tree at: https://linktr.ee/glofernwolfe

Wattle Tree Press is an independent publisher
located on the picturesque Central Coast of Australia.
WTP believes that everyone has a story (or two) within them
and aims to bring Aussie storytelling to the wider world.

Their growing catalogue can be found at:

www.wattletreepress.com

www.ingramcontent.com/pod-product-compliance
Lightning Source LLC
Chambersburg PA
CBHW061031100726
47911CB00006B/152